The

SUBURB
BEYOND
✦ THE ✦
STARS

The SUBURB BEYOND ⇥★⇤ THE STARS

The Norumbegan Quartet

Volume 2

M. T. ANDERSON

★ SCHOLASTIC INC. ★

New York Toronto London Auckland
Sydney Mexico City New Delhi Hong Kong

This book was originally published
by Scholastic Press in 2010.

ISBN 978-0-545-13883-3

12 11 10 9 8 7 6 5 4 3 2 1   11 12 13 14 15 16/0

Printed in the U.S.A.   40
First paperback printing, March 2011

The text was set in Excelsior.
The display type is P22 Parrish.

Book design by Steve Scott

To N.
in the house of hair.

ONE

Brian Thatz noticed he was being followed as he walked from his cello lesson to the old office building where he played interdimensional games.

At first, it was just a feeling that someone was watching. He pushed his glasses more securely onto the bridge of his nose and looked around. No one seemed suspicious. There were some other students with violins and guitars hopping down the steps of the music school. A crossing guard. Two women in high heels, wobbling on the brick sidewalks.

So Brian kept walking, dragging his cello. Sometimes he wished he'd chosen a smaller instrument. Even the viola would have been better.

But there was the feeling again — like someone lightly touching his back, a gaze lingering on his collar, on his neck, on the fringe of hair coming out from under his baseball cap.

He frowned and glanced at the windows he passed to see if they reflected signs of movement.

1

Nothing. But the feeling persisted. He kept going for a block or two, then turned.

This time, he saw who was following him.

The man wore a camel-hair overcoat and carried nothing in his hands. His face, at a distance, was a violent and bloody red.

Brian loved to read old detective stories with names like *The Gimleyhough Diamond*, *A Wee Case of Murder*, and *What Goes Up*. In these books, people were always being hired to follow other people. They called it "shadowing," and the creeps who shadowed were called "shadows" or "tails."

Brian's shadow was not very good at remaining unseen. The man clearly was used to following sly, nimble victims who slipped through crowds and darted down alleyways. He wasn't particularly gifted when it came to lurking behind a stocky boy struggling down the street with a cello. The shadow had to make frequent stops so he wouldn't walk right past Brian. He had to pretend he was interested in birds.

There were plenty of birds. It was early summer in Cambridge, and the Common was alive with them. An oak shuffled with finches. Brian saw the tail pause about fifteen feet back to shield his eyes and admire them. The man's red face was riddled with old pockmarks, scumbled like cottage cheese.

While the tail watched the finches, Brian decided to make a break for the subway station. He lifted his cello — cranking up his elbows — and hopped across the puddles. For blocks, he puffed and hauled.

Even he could tell his burst of speed was pathetic. College students taking a brisk stroll walked right past him. Bicyclists nearly ran into him. The tail kept ambling along across the Common, fascinated by jays, looking fitfully at the dirty sky, slightly embarrassed to be so visible.

The tail followed Brian past a bus stop, past an old graveyard, past a church and a drunken busker playing the accordion. The man followed him past a newsstand and down the escalators to the T, Boston's subway.

When the train pulled into the station and the doors hissed and rattled open, Brian lunged into the nearest car. He rested his back against one of the poles and twisted his neck to look out. The tail was headed along the platform, straight for the same car. The man stepped in at the other end and stood staring, unperturbed. No longer, apparently, so interested in birds.

"Ashmont train," the voice on the loudspeaker said. "Stand clear of the doors. Stand clear."

Brian flung himself toward the doors as they shut. He hauled his cello behind him.

His cello got tangled with the pole and seat. Brian tripped and almost fell.

"Whoa," said a kid in a hoodie, gripping Brian's shoulder. "Steady."

Now there was no way he could get off in time. The doors were closed. The train pulled out of the station. The tail stared down the car as if Brian were a natural event he was watching. They all raced through tunnels, wheels screaming.

Brian knew who might have sent the man to shadow

3

him. Nearly a year before, Brian and his friend Gregory had gone on a strange adventure in the northern woods of Vermont. They had found themselves the pawns in an ancient, supernatural game that led to mountain-tops, caverns, and ogres. When Brian won the Game, he had also won the right to oversee the Game's next round. Now he suspected that the tail who now stood a few feet from him had been sent by the Thusser, the elfin nation that had lost that contest. Perhaps they were trying to gain some advantage.

Maybe this man, the shadow with clotted cheeks, was sent to find out where Brian's workshop was hidden. Several days a week after school, Brian went to an old office building, where he and Gregory set up the next round of the Game, making up riddles and designing monstrosities. Maybe the Thusser were trying to catch a glimpse of Brian's plans.

Or maybe they sought revenge.

Brian thought carefully about what to do. He prided himself on always being rational and logical. He knew that in a few stops, the T train would shoot briefly above-ground. It would cross a bridge over the Charles River, and for a minute or so, his phone would work. He decided he would call Gregory and tell him he wasn't going to the workshop today. He'd ask Gregory to meet him at a different stop instead, and they'd both just walk back to Brian's house. That way they wouldn't be giving the tail any new information. There was nothing secret about Brian's own address. It could be found by anyone with a phone book and thumbs.

4

Brian took his phone out of his pocket. He waited for the train to rise out of the tunnel. He anxiously flipped the phone open and closed, open and closed.

As the subway neared the mouth of the tunnel, he speed-dialed Gregory. He held the phone up to his ear. It was ringing.

The tail watched Brian call. His blotched lips started to move, as if he whispered information to someone who couldn't be seen. He closed his eyes.

The train rolled across a dark granite bridge between black turrets. The city of Boston was spread out on its hill. Sailboats were on the river, and people were jogging along the banks. Brian knew he only had about forty-five seconds. The phone was still ringing.

The train stopped at the Charles Street station. People got on and off, hefting backpacks. Brian hunched over the phone, shielding his face with his cello, which rested between his legs and the grasp bar. The phone rang on.

Then, finally, someone answered.

"Hey," said Gregory's voice. "Listen to this."

"No, Gregory," whispered Brian urgently. "There's someone following me. Can you meet me at —"

There was a squalling noise at the other end of the phone, a vicious hissing, a crash.

"Did you hear that?" Gregory said. "I put the cat on my dad's turntable. Like, for vinyl."

"Yeah. Gregory, I'm being followed. One of the Thusser, I think. Can you meet me at —"

There was another sharp *hiss*, another *thump*.

5

Gregory came back on the phone. "Side B," he explained.

"Gregory, *listen*!"

"How did people ever think that was a high-definition sound system?"

"Gregory, I need you to meet me at —"

The train sped back underground. Brian shouted the name of a stop, but his phone had already lost its signal.

He was on his own.

He hated that. It was much easier to be brave when there was someone else to rely on. Brian was used to relying on Gregory. Nervously rocking the handle of his cello case back and forth, he considered what he was going to do.

He was supposed to change trains at the next stop, Park Street, where a lot of people stepped off the train or on. But he stayed put, half an eye turned to watch his pursuer. He thought to himself grimly that this was not the first time the Thusser had tailed him on a train. That was how the Game had begun. It had ended with the Thusser agent trying to kill Brian on the floor of a subterranean cathedral. Just thinking about it made Brian panic.

He waited two stops. Then, at the third, just as people were scrambling for seats and the doors were about to close — at the very last minute — Brian seized his cello and forced his way out onto the platform.

The rush-hour crowd was all around him. They still fought to get onto the train. He dodged between them, yanking the cello clumsily behind him. He looked back and saw the camel-hair shadow shoving his way out through

6

the doors, peering around the station. Brian ducked and, slanting the cello like artillery, moved along the wall. He found a column and hid behind it.

He waited. The train pulled away. Another train pulled in. He heard the doors open and people get out. He heard the subterranean voice of the conductor announce the line and the next station. The doors shut. The train moved on.

There was now an awful wailing. It was not the train shrieking on the rails. It was human. Carefully, Brian peered around the column.

The platform was almost empty. The tail stood, looking at Brian's column. Between them stood a freckled man with a baby in a backpack. The noise was the baby bawling, red faced.

The four of them stood for a long time that way. The shadow couldn't do a thing with a witness standing there. The baby kept screaming. Its face was turning purplish. The freckled father glanced at the man in the camel-hair coat, glanced at Brian. He looked nervous. He could tell something was going on.

Brian stared back at the shadow defiantly. Or at least he hoped he looked defiant. In truth, he was desperately agonizing over how he would lose the man while still dragging his cello with him — trying to dodge through crowds, up and down subway stairs, and along the sidewalks of Brookline.

The baby sobbed on.

The man in the camel-hair coat gave Brian a final, hateful look, then turned and walked off. He trudged up the stairs.

Brian's shoulders sagged with relief. His cello dipped. He realized that it had been sticking out from behind the column the whole time, completely obvious. He was awful at hiding.

He pulled the cello around the pillar and stood with his back against the concrete, waiting for another train. He tried to shut out the baby's anguished wail, which blared and boomed in the tunnel.

He was almost relieved when the baby stopped to gag and cough.

But it was at that moment that he heard the shadow talking to people on the stairs. "You can't go down there," said the shadow. "Police. Sorry, ma'am. Police. This station is closed. We're having a situation."

A woman said, "I have to go pick up salmon."

"You won't be leaving from this station, ma'am. We're engaged in an activity."

Why, thought Brian, *is he shooing people away?*

And then he looked at the freckled man, the baby in the backpack. The man was walking toward him, head sinking down between his shoulders. The baby screamed, red, blotchy, and bald.

No one was coming down the stairs. There wouldn't be any witnesses.

Brian's heart swung a beat and began to pound.

The baby's mouth spread wide, too wide for any human mouth. Though it was an infant, it had rows and rows and rows of teeth.

It looked very hungry.

TWO

Brian had to get by the man and the demon baby. He had to get up the steps. He grabbed his cello and then he thought, *Wait. I'll have to leave the cello.* This was not easy for him to do. He and the cello had been through a lot together: melancholy sonatas . . . terrifying recitals. But still, that didn't mean they had to die together. He left it leaning, darted to the side, dashed for the exit.

The freckled man put out an arm and veered toward him.

Brian saw he wouldn't make it to the steps. He skidded to a stop and dropped low like he had seen basketball players do. He hovered, waiting to see which way the freckled man would move.

The freckled man was not a human organism. His face was crumpling into something creased and alien, and it was clear that the infant on his back was no separate infant but another head on the same body, a hump,

9

another mouth to feed. The baby was not squinting — it didn't have eyes. Just that wide, saw-toothed mouth.

The man-infant was, for a moment, poised like Brian, knees bent, hands low. And then it was on all fours. Arms and legs were bending in ways that no human limb could twist without snapping.

The creature was rearing to pounce.

Brian tried to make a break for it. He took a few thudding steps to the left. The monster countered, its infant mouth still screaming and sloppy.

The beast's father-mouth snarled and snapped. The baby-head, now bloated and distorted, rocked and howled. The monster paced forward. Brian stepped back.

It was now or never. Brian turned and ran past his pillar, past his cello, to a service door in the tunnel. He tugged the handle.

Locked.

The monster had not moved, but smiled a curiously human smile and began to prowl forward, elbows out.

Brian didn't like the look of those two mouths, nor the gnarled fingers that tapped along the concrete floor.

There was no place to run. There was no more platform.

Brian jumped down onto the tracks. Mice scattered as he hit the sooty gravel.

Farther down the tunnel, he saw the light from the inbound platform. If he could just make it there, there would be people — witnesses — maybe help.

So he ran.

Gravel chiseled at his shoes, spattered behind him. He

10

heard the *thunk* as the beast threw itself down after him and began to lope forward. He heard it gaining.

Down the tunnel, at the inbound platform, there was not only light, not only the sound of people milling, but music. Brian could hear a man with a guitar, warbling, "You put me high upon a pedestal... so high that I could —"

The monster was at Brian's side. It was still twenty feet to the music, the light, the crowd. And now the monster was in front of him.

It grinned and lifted one of its emaciated claws. Its clothes were in shreds from its transformation. Its baby-mouth was huge and warping with its cries. The beast was ready to finish him off.

Brian suddenly had an idea. A last chance.

The baby-maw coughed and drooled wet cheese, milk curdled with the blood of some previous victim.

"Uh — uh — okay," said Brian. "Come on."

The monster pounced.

And at the same time, Brian hurtled backward, swinging his arms. He straddled the electrified third rail — one foot on either side of it — and thudded back, terrified he'd tumble. He took a chance that the creature wasn't aware of human ways. He bet that a monster sent by the Thusser wouldn't know that through the subway's third rail ran a thousand volts of electricity.

The beast paced toward him as he scrambled away. It swung its heads from side to side.

Digging his heels into the black gravel, Brian kept staggering backward.

The monster slipped forward, raising a bony claw to maul him. Brian shrank away — pivoted — felt the claw swipe —

— and miss —

— and hit the rail.

The alien beast's body arched. The bulging father-eyes blinked once.

The baby-mouth gave a furious yowl.

And then the thing fell and began to spasm on the tracks. Its back arched further. Its feet flailed.

Brian watched in horror.

Then he saw a train was coming — at first, just light on the wall and a barreling racket.

He scampered toward the outbound platform, where he had come from.

He pulled himself up.

The train appeared in the tunnel. Brian was sitting on the yellow strip near the platform's edge. His whole body still stung with alarm.

As the train pulled into the station, Brian stood up, shaking, next to his instrument case. The doors opened. People trooped out.

And a few seconds later, Brian got on, lugging his cello, and headed to meet Gregory. There was nothing following him now.

Except the knowledge that he was hunted, and that whatever sought him out would not stop until he was dead.

THREE

Many centuries ago, when the people of Europe still dressed in pelts and scavenged like animals, back when queens pulled birds apart with their teeth, and kings lived in wooden shacks they called feasting halls, a race of sublime, elfin creatures dwelled in the hills. These creatures held court in gemmed ballrooms and delighted themselves with subtle games and whispery fantasias played on instruments of silver. They were reasonably fond of the human animal, though the humans tended to smell bad, eat too much, cry about angels, and leave their droppings on the floor. When the human beasts started to multiply, however, many of the elfin race felt there was no longer enough room for their airy castles and subterranean cities in the hills of Europe, and so a party of them set out for the New World, having read that the human population there was more scarce and not so given to delving in the ground and knocking down sacred groves.

They crossed the Atlantic Ocean in their hovering coracles and galleons. In the mountains of what is now Vermont, they founded a fabled kingdom called Norumbega. Beneath the hills they built palaces and cathedrals and the City of Gargoyles, with stone streets and squares where they held their weird games and rituals for many centuries. They lived there happily — practicing falconry in the forests, holding sub-aquatic jousts in mountain lakes, playing golf with greens and holes in other worlds — until one day when another eldritch race, the Thusser, came to challenge them.

The Thusser wanted to rule over the Empire of Norumbega. They could tell it was built upon an inter-dimensional rift of great power. They wanted that power for themselves. They felt they would use it more cleverly than the Norumbegans, who spent their days strapping themselves to kites and designing beautiful boots. The Thusser decided they would take the kingdom by force. They began a devastating war, a siege of the mountain.

The Norumbegans plated their highest peaks in metal and sent out airborne warships and dragonauts in goggles to drop bombs on the Thusser Horde crowded below. The Thusser built huge guns and marched in inexorable waves toward the battlements, hurling shot as large as hills at the armored summit.

The siege would have gone on for years and would have exhausted both parties if they hadn't come to a curious stalemate. The Norumbegans were losing — being somewhat too frivolous for a sustained siege. They called a cease-fire and parleyed with the Thusser, complaining

14

that they were finding warfare (as they said) "too too dreadfully human." The idea of making vital political and economic decisions based on how much enemy flesh one could ravage reminded them too much of the animals they'd left behind in the muck of the Old World. It was absurd. They wanted, instead, to decide the conflict on the basis of a much more arbitrary and trivial system. They wanted to play a game.

Each generation, two human pawns were chosen to enter into some kind of a labyrinth. One (without knowing it) represented the Norumbegans; the other (also without knowing it) represented the Thusser. Each round, one team or the other would claim victory — and whichever human won would devise the puzzles and traps for the next round. At the end of all the rounds, the fate of the kingdom would be decided. Either the Norumbegans would take possession again, or the Thusser would sweep in and make it their own.

In the meantime, while the Game was played, Norumbega would remain unoccupied by either team. The Norumbegans themselves went into exile in another world. The Thusser watched jealously over the Game from their haunts.

And now it was Brian Thatz's turn to create a round of the Game. He had won a victory for the Norumbegans. It was up to him to build a world into which he would, in several years, have to lead some hapless pair of players.

When Brian and Gregory had played the Game, the whole thing had been arranged by Gregory's cousin Prudence. She was a fan of Gothic novels, so she had

15

created a round full of menacing servants, monsters in the woods, and mansions with turrets.

Brian, on the other hand, loved old detective novels — hard-boiled stories in which sad men in trench coats leaned against brick walls, coughing on phlegm and watching the silhouettes of lovers on the window shades above. So he had decided he would create a supernatural mystery story, a set of strange puzzles that would lead his players — whoever they turned out to be — through the mean streets of Boston, down darkened alleyways, and into an underworld populated by gangster minotaurs and blond dames with wings.

His workshop for the Game was a series of rooms in an old, unused art deco office building. It had been rented for him by an agent of the Norumbegans, a bitter elfin mechanic named Wee Sniggleping. Wee Sniggleping was in charge of arranging things according to Brian's specifications and the complicated Rules. In his mountaintop workshop, he was building gangsters and molls, toughs and stooges, so they could eventually populate Brian's round. When completed and installed, they would swagger and growl like real people.

Wee Sniggleping and Brian had not yet refinished the office building. Above the front door, the stucco shadow of old lettering still read WORLDWIDE INDUSTRIAL BATTER CO. Inside, the afternoon light shone through cracked windows into a ruin of fallen plaster, graffiti, and chipped marble facing. Upstairs, there were floors of metal filing cabinets with drawers torn out, hallways where the wooden paneling had been smashed, and wires yanked out of the walls.

But there was one office that had already been restored and prepared for the Game. On the pebbled glass window of the door was freshly painted NATE FLOCKTON — PRIVATE EYE. And inside was Brian's headquarters.

He and Gregory had turned it for the moment into a kind of clubhouse. There were huge ornate desks from a century before and some giant fake ferns. Gregory had hung plastic parrots and cockatoos on perches from the ceiling. The two found some horrible paintings in the garbage — Technicolor dogs with their tongues out and landscapes that looked like the surface of Venus after a neon storm — and hung them unevenly on the walls. Brian had brought over some boxes of his favorite books and an encyclopedia that he'd stuck in some church bookshelves.

The upper half of a mechanical secretary — her lower half was just a set of metal struts — greeted them whenever they walked in. "Why, hi there, boys," she would say. "Mr. Flockton ain't in. You want I should take a message, or you okay just cooling your heels 'til he gets back from whatever filthy joint he's sunk in today?" There was no Mr. Flockton yet — Wee Sniggleping still had to build him, as well as twelve other assorted cops and crime lords. Even the secretary, Minnie, was still in her early stages and could say only a few things — but it was always exciting for Brian to see the world he had planned come together.

17

Now, however, Brian was pacing around in the inner office while Gregory sat on the old couch, listening to his story.

"You don't think the Thusser were trying to find this place?" Gregory asked.

"At first I thought that, but now I'm not sure," said Brian. "I don't think it makes sense. I know that they're talking to Sniggleping and the Speculant about all the stuff we're doing here. They must know where our head-quarters are."

"Maybe they don't."

"I don't think it was just about tailing me."

"Yeah, the tail. You said he had blotchy cheeks?"

"Like he'd had some kind of disease."

Brian looked down at Gregory. Gregory was smiling. Exasperated, Brian said, "What? What's funny?"

"Your tail has pimply cheeks. You have pimply cheeks on your tail."

"Gregory!" Brian protested. "I was almost killed."

"I'm sorry," Gregory said. He tried to drop his smile.

"Stop joking."

"I've stopped. Look. Here's me serious."

Gregory took on the expression of an undertaker who'd once dreamed of dancing on Broadway.

Brian frowned and absently knocked on one of the encyclopedias, trying to calm down. Sometimes he hated it that Gregory never took anything seriously. It made him feel like he was some dull boy in knee socks, some twerp bringing down a great party by complaining about almost being killed. He knew that if Gregory had been

18

confronted with squalling evil on the T, there'd be a great story with lots of sly jokes, and it would sound like Gregory was a hero, calm and cool. And if it could be told to other people, kids would be gathered around Gregory like they always were, boys slapping his arms, girls touching their hair, smiling.

And of course, Brian realized, he himself would be one of the people who'd laugh at Gregory's jokes. Because that was what was great about Gregory: He never gave up. He never stopped laughing. He balanced Brian's thoughtful frown. That's what made the two of them a good team.

Brian sighed and knocked again on the encyclopedias. He said, "I don't think that they were just trying to follow me. I think their plan all along was to get me alone and kill me."

"Are you kidding? You really think they would have killed you? Completely?"

"Yes, Gregory! They tried! I'm telling you, this monster really was inches from tearing me apart!"

"Wow." Gregory nodded. "It's great that you thought of that third rail trick." He shook his head. He looked genuinely uneasy.

Brian said, "I'm lucky I didn't trip or something. I would've died, too. I can't even think about it."

"I know. Dude."

"It's so weird. I can't tell my parents. They'd think the whole thing was crazy. Here I am being threatened, and I can't tell anyone. Except you. And maybe Prudence. She'd understand."

"What are we going to do?"

Brian was glad Gregory had said *we*. He replied, "We have to talk to Prudence."

"I haven't heard from her in a week or so."

"I know," said Brian. "I've tried on e-mail and the mirror. She doesn't respond." He sat down heavily on the couch. "Now I'm worried about her, too. Gregory, what if they got her?"

"Why would they 'get her'?" asked Gregory. "She's no longer involved with the Game. She was in charge of the last round. And there's no reason for them to attack you, either. You're just the, I don't know, referee or something."

Brian insisted, "We have to get through to her. She's the only one who might know what to do. I'm terrified even to walk home."

"I'll go with you . . . as long as I don't have to carry the cello."

Brian bit his lip. "If we can't get through to Prudence in a couple of days, we're going to have to go up there and see what's happened to her."

Gregory nodded.

As Brian dialed Prudence, and listened to the phone ring and ring and go to the message, they looked around their office — the rubber plants, the glass-eyed cockatoos. Suddenly it didn't look as cozy as it once had. They were aware of how much of the building was empty and how quickly evening was falling outside.

Usually Brian and Prudence wrote notes to each other every few days. Brian was working his way through the huge tomes that explained the Game's Rules. Though they had been translated into English at some point in the last century, they were not easy to read. Quite often, Brian sent Prudence e-mails like the following:

From: bthatz@brooklinehigh.edu
To: theprude@norumbega.net
Subject: The Manual of Fouls

Hi, Prudence,

Sorry to ask another question, but I'm really confused. On page 52 of the Manual of Fouls there's a chart of "Powers Reserved to Tertiary Personae" and I don't really get the restrictions on movement. How are those equations supposed to be used?

I feel really stupid. I'm worried that I just can't do this. I'll never understand all this stuff.

Brian

And Prudence would write back things like:

From: theprude@norumbega.net
To: bthatz@brooklinehigh.edu
Subject: Re: The Manual of Fouls

Hey, Squirt!

Who in this world actually understands what they're doing? I don't. I just spent forty-five minutes trying to sort laundry. They tell you not to mix darks and lights, but WHAT DO YOU DO WITH TARTAN? It is mixed with itself.

Even worse: The official Norumbegan tartan contains a stripe of some color invisible to the human eye. It's a color called "dweomer-pale." *What does it look like?* sez you. *How the heck should I know?* sez I. It's invisible to the human eye. I just don't want it to run and muck up my burgundy.

The skirt's wool. I guess I should probably wash it by itself anyway.

Oh. Wait. You don't care.

What I'm trying to say, Scooter, is that we're all confused, and you're smarter than most of us. You won the Game for a reason — and your plan for the next round is amazing. I love the thought you're putting into this mystery scenario. It's going to be incredibly cool. I can tell that Gregory is green with envy. It shall rock. Don't forget that a lot of the details you're worried about will be taken care of by Snig and the Speculant and their cronies a few years from now. You'll have plenty of time to read the manuals.

So stop biting the rope. You will be fine.

Okay. To answer your particular question about powers of movement, what I remember goes sumfin like this. . . .

And then she'd tell him what she knew.

But Brian hadn't heard from her in at least a week. She hadn't responded to any of his recent questions. He'd assumed that she was just busy.

Gregory occasionally had a little back-and-forth with her, teasing her about how boring she was, making jokes about how Brian was in love with her. Not for a while, though. There hadn't been a peep from her.

22

Brian was worried now. Very worried.

He and Gregory didn't laugh or joke as they locked up the office. ("Night, boys," said the automaton at the desk. "I'll tell Nate you were snooping in his donut drawer, soon as he gets back.") They didn't talk as they made their way through the dark interior of the Industrial Batter Co. Building, kicking their way through plaster trash.

Gregory walked out the front door first. He looked around carefully before he stepped away and let Brian out into the light of the street. He walked with Brian to the Thatzes' apartment building, and left Brian there. Throughout the evening, they exchanged nervous messages to check on each other.

Even at home, Brian didn't feel safe. His family's apartment was always noisy. It was right over a main road, so all night, there were cars and the upshifting of trucks. The noise of the traffic meant that Brian's parents always had to yell, which they would have done anyway, since they were those kind of people: friendly and loud.

Usually the grinding wash of the graveyard-shift commute put Brian to sleep as if it were some familiar river. The shouting of his parents from room to room ("Hey! Have you read this article on greens? Why don't we eat more greens?") was usually reassuring.

But now Brian heard only the sounds masked by the traffic. He heard things creak and tick. He heard what might be footsteps in the early hours of the morning. He was sure that something was out to get him.

He thought of the monsters he'd encountered in the Vermont woods — the Basement Lurker, like a childhood nightmare, hardly glimpsed save for the red jaws, the claws that snatched; the blind ogre Snarth, who fumbled through subterranean depths; and, most horrifying of all, Gelt the Winnower (haunter of Brian's dreams for almost a year now), some production of the Thusser, a body like a man's with spikes driven through it and, where each spike hit flesh, a long, silver cord that snaked out, sentient. Gelt felt through those cords — and could use them to snare, strangle, and dismember.

The little ticks of the building settling . . . the trickle of water through pipes as neighbors flushed . . . the grunt of flexing floorboards . . . all of these sounded to Brian like Gelt or one of his awful brethren feeling his way through the dark apartment, lips moving, eyes blank. The clock glowed. It shifted from 3:31 to 3:32.

Brian lay on his back and stared at the ceiling. He did not have the courage to turn onto his side.

✳ ✳ ✳

Gregory walked the rest of the way home, peering anxiously into bushes. He hoped he wasn't monster bait. Brian had won the Game, after all — Gregory hadn't.

At home, he couldn't concentrate on his homework. He kept texting Brian to make sure nothing had happened — nothing had kicked through a window or clambered up the fire escape.

Gregory cycled through Prudence's recent e-mails. No hint of a trip. No mention that she was shipping out to Turkey for a few weeks of sunshine and döner kebab. Nothing but bright, cheery reports of cooking triumphs and plumbing disasters. A few rude barbs about Gregory hitting puberty "like a stinkbug on a windshield."

Gregory tried her again on the phone. No answer. He talked to his parents. They hadn't heard anything from her.

If something had happened to her, he realized with a sinking heart, it had happened without her seeing that it was coming.

He sank down onto his desk chair and crossed his arms. Prudence was Gregory's favorite family member. Most of the fam came from Connecticut; they spent their Thanksgivings comparing the first-class cabins of international airlines and trading tips about where to buy swordfish steaks or boar butter in "the City," by which they meant New York. Prudence was the only one with a sense of humor. Well, she was the only one who'd laughed when Gregory rigged the roast turkey to scream.

When Gregory pictured himself older — an old man — sitting at the head of the table with his own children and grandchildren cowering in front of his own screaming turkey, he pictured their Auntie Prude at the same table, after a lifetime of ribbing each other at weddings and irritating the cousins. They'd have jokes, passwords, stories they could tell.

Weeks often went by without her calling. So maybe nothing was wrong. Maybe she just wasn't answering her phone. But maybe something awful *had* happened, and it had fallen upon her so quickly and so savagely she didn't have time to call for help.

Gregory sat at his desk and played with pennies. The night outside his windows got thicker.

✳ ✳ ✳

Brian was exhausted the next day. He'd hardly slept. At Newbury Comics, where kids tended to gather, Brian watched as Gregory held court like usual, surrounded by friends. Crowds were Gregory's natural element. When some new bud made a crack about Brian Thatz looking like he was about to nod off, Brian just stood blinking and feeling ashamed and not knowing what to say. Gregory came to his rescue. "Cut Bri-Bri some slack. He had a rough day yesterday."

"Playing his *cello*?"

"No," said Gregory. "Fighting off a two-headed monster in the subway. It's a tough neighborhood."

"He's chubby for a master of the martial arts."

"He used his cunning wiles," said Gregory, tapping his forehead. "He electrocuted the monster on the third rail. Three rails, two heads, one winner." He yanked up Brian's hand in victory.

And everyone grinned. They thought Gregory was a card.

Brian blushed. He was grateful. He didn't know why it was that he could take care of himself when clawed by a two-headed monster, but he was helpless when it came to crowds of Gregory's other friends — one head each.

Regardless, Brian could tell that Gregory was worried about him — he even got seconds for Brian at lunch, like he thought his friend needed to keep up his strength.

Just after lunch, they headed over to their headquarters to try to get Sniggleping or Prudence on the two-way mirror.

The two boys clanked through the broken-down foyer of the building and trudged up the stairs. Light fell in through the huge windows and lit the dust in the air.

"I told my parents we might go up and see Prudence this weekend," Gregory told Brian. "They said that was cool with them. I lied and told them she'd invited us."

"I have to ask my parents," Brian replied. "As long as we're back by Sunday night, I don't think it will be a problem."

Gregory asked soberly, "*Will* we be back by Sunday night?"

"I hope we don't have to go at all," said Brian. He turned the key in the lock of the office and they walked in.

"Howdy, Minnie, love of my life," Gregory greeted the automaton, saluting her with one hand and blowing a kiss with his other.

"Why, hi there, boys," said Minnie, winking slyly, as she always did. "Mr. Flockton ain't in. You want I should take a message, or you okay just cooling your heels 'til he gets back from whatever filthy joint he's sunk in today?"

27

"Thanks, Minnie," said Brian, heading for the inner office, Gregory close behind him.

Minnie smiled, picked up her letter opener, and stabbed at Brian.

Gregory yelled, *"Brian!"* and leaped — grabbing her arm.

Minnie fought, rocking Gregory back and forth as he gripped the flesh of her wrist. He could feel the beams and cogs beneath the skin. "Why, hi there, boys," she said. "Mr. Flockton ain't — Why, hi there, boys, Mr. Flockton ain't — Why, hi there, boys, the Game is over. Why, hi there, boys, the Game is over, boys. Why, boys, the Game —"

She jabbed. Brian gripped her upper shoulder. He and Gregory yanked, and with a jolt, they pulled off their secretary's arm.

In their hands, still wired, it kept bending and writhing, trying to stab but without purchase. Her fingers, dolled up, were wrapped around the letter opener's hilt, white with tension.

"Why, hi there, boys. Why, hi there, boys. Why, hi there, boys. Here's a message for you. Here's a message for you."

"From who?" Brian shouted. "Who's it from, Minnie?"

"Here's a message. Here's a message. Here's a message."

"What's the message?" Brian screamed. The arm bucked in his hands. "What is it?"

"The knife. The Game is over, boys. Why, hi there, boys. Why, hi. Why, hi there. The knife. The Game is over. Why . . ."

28

Her eyes went blank. The arm stopped struggling.

Brian stepped quickly behind her and felt for the plate in Minnie's back where her windup key would be inserted.

"Be careful," Gregory warned.

"Get me a screwdriver," said Brian.

"I mean be careful because that's my own true love you're pawing up."

"How did she get reprogrammed?" Brian demanded. No one answered.

Gregory went to the inner office and returned with a screwdriver.

Brian took off the plate in Minnie's back. Inside were gears and springs. Brian didn't know much about how the magical automatons worked, but he knew that if he snapped the spring that the key wound, she couldn't start up again on her own. She'd have to be fixed first by Sniggleping.

He yanked her spring.

"Let's call up Sniggleping on the mirror," said Gregory. "He made her. He'll know how someone could reprogram her."

"Something's going very wrong," said Brian. "None of this should be happening. We're not competing right now."

They went into the inner office, where their communications mirror hung, an old 1920s thing in a glamorous Bakelite frame. Brian touched it and said the Cantrip of Activation. Then he said Sniggleping's name.

"Come on, Sniggleping," Brian said. "Be there today."

Prudence had taught Brian a few simple spells he'd

29

need to run the Game. The Cantrip of Activation was one of them. It acted as a toggle switch for many Norumbegan artifacts, turning them on or off.

The mirror was crowded with the boys' faces. As the Cantrip took hold, the mirror image faded; the glass slowly frosted. The faces turned white and eyeless. Brian's glasses were dim loops of gray. As the boys watched and waited for Sniggleping to appear, Gregory said, "I'm going to get Prudence to teach me the Cantrip of Activation, too."

"I can try to teach you again," Brian offered. "Anytime."

"It's just one word, right? Come on. How hard can it be?"

"Well, yeah . . . but . . . no, it's not just one word, exactly," said Brian. "It's a set of things you have to think about, too."

"We tried before. I got the spoken part right."

"You have to clear your mind and think about the right things. Otherwise, you're just saying stuff."

Gregory looked miffed. "Why does Prudence teach you all these things and not me?"

"She — I'm sure she'd teach you, too. You said you didn't want to learn. You said it was boring."

"Now I don't think it's boring."

"Last time I tried to teach you, you got all . . . you got mad."

"Maybe I'm dumb."

"You're not dumb."

"Never mind. It's just that Prude pays more attention to you just because you won the Game."

Brian's washed-out face creased with concern in the fading mirror. "She doesn't pay more attention —"

"Yeah, yeah. Where's Snig?" said Gregory irritably.

Brian and Gregory looked through themselves, and dimly saw Sniggleping's workshop in the mountains of Vermont.

And abruptly, their little spat was forgotten.

For this is what they saw: Sniggleping's workshop was empty. Not a thing remained. It had always been crammed with plans and tools and half-built heads and entrails spun on spools. Now there was nothing but an expanse of floor, an empty balcony.

"What happened?" Gregory gasped.

"He's gone. He took everything with him."

"No," said Gregory. "He didn't leave by choice. Look at the floor. The strip of light."

"What do you mean?"

"His door must be open. He left his door just flapping open. He wouldn't have left the place unlocked. Not if he left by himself."

"You're right," said Brian, unbelieving. "Someone's taken him. They must have. Someone broke in and dragged him off."

"Okay," said Gregory, pressing his fingers together. "Wee Snig's gone. Prudence is missing."

"Someone programmed Minnie to kill. And I was attacked by a monster on the T."

31

"Something's *seriously* gone wrong. What are we going to do?"

Brian exhaled heavily. They knew what needed to be done. And it scared them both.

"Let's get packing," Brian said. "We're going to Vermont."

FOUR

As the train crossed iron bridges, Brian gazed out the window at the millponds and sumac thickets below.

"I'm looking forward to seeing the mountains again," Gregory said.

"And Kalgrash," said Brian. "He'll be there."

"Oh, yeah. Sure. Great." Gregory sounded sarcastic.

Brian smiled. "I like Kalgrash."

"I like the little guy fine. Of all the people who have ever attacked me with a battle-ax, he's my favorite."

"It was his job."

"I'm not sure you should forgive someone for trying to ax you just because they were programmed to."

"He didn't try to ax us. He just blocked us."

"With an ax."

Brian pressed his lips together. "And can you please not remind him about the programming? When we see him? No one likes to hear they're just clockwork. Remember: Sniggleping built him to feel stuff."

33

"All right. Okay. Fine." Gregory took a bite of some kind of fruit leather so tough that his face warped when he chewed. "You know, it's a little weird to say this, but overall, I'm actually ready to go back. I mean, because of the adventure. It really was kind of cool, with the forest and the mountains and, yeah, the troll, even. It felt like we were actually *doing* something."

"It was like we'd been waiting for it all our lives," Brian agreed. He looked out the window at passing burbs. He wished that he actually felt that way — that he didn't just feel like they were galloping into a trap.

"We're going to do this," said Gregory. "We're going to find Prudence and sort this all out. Right?"

"Right," said Brian. He wasn't convinced. "I hope so."

"Don't say 'I hope so.' Think positive. Say 'Yes.' Come on. Through your megaphone: *'Why, certainly, my good sir!'* It's an adventure, dude."

Gregory's enthusiasm was infectious. They were both swept up by the feeling of the task to be completed. They talked about the places they'd visited in the forest . . . the paths through dark glades, the interdimensional clock keeping time for some other world, Kalgrash's cozy burrow underneath the old stone bridge, and the Haunted Hunting Grounds, where specters of the Norumbegan court still sought their prey.

They had stood on top of the mountain, looking out over that forest — looking past Grendle Manor and the steeples of distant churches, far-flung fields, the trees in their last brown leaves before the coming of snow from the North — and they had vowed that they would never forget any of it, they would never give in to suits and company coffee mugs and nine-to-five. Nothing could be the same after the magical wood.

Brian said, "Anything can happen in that forest."

"Yeah. Who knows — we might even survive."

Brian allowed himself to smile. "It's possible."

They got off the train in Gerenford, Vermont, Gregory dragging his luggage behind him on wheels. Brian was carrying only a backpack.

The town green looked much the same as it had the year before: same church, same plain nineteenth-century houses, same statue of the same founder holding up the same skinned rabbit. It was busier, though. In the fall, he and Gregory had been picked up here by horse and carriage. It didn't look the same in the summer, with parents tipping back their strollers to hop sidewalks and girls straggling past eating Chipwiches. It didn't look like a mad-uncle-in-a-buggy town anymore.

In the absence of a carriage, they had called ahead and arranged for a taxi to take them to Prudence's house. It was waiting for them when they arrived. It was a station wagon with the word *Taxi* Scotch-taped to its window.

It drove them out of town. They couldn't speak freely about magic and skulduggery in front of the driver.

"I hope she's all right," said Gregory. He was clearly getting more nervous as they got closer. Trees passed the windows.

Brian looked at his friend with concern. "She's your favorite relative, isn't she?" he asked.

"Of course. She laughed at my screaming turkey." He

35

murmured, "She can't be gone. There's got to be some normal explanation we haven't thought of yet."

They were not headed to Grendle Manor. That house had been some kind of magical construction, built as carefully as a wedding cake especially for the Game, and it had disintegrated when it was no longer needed. After the round was won, Prudence had moved back into her old house, a sixties ranch-style home on a dirt road at the base of Norumbega Mountain.

That was where they were headed when they drove through the gates of a new suburban development. The car passed streets of replicated, generous houses. "Wow," said Gregory. "She said there were some new streets near her, but this is a lot of houses."

"It's only been here for a little while," the taxi driver offered from the front seat. "Kind of a new development. Rumbling Elk Haven. My sister lives here."

"We camped here when it was woods," said Brian.

"It was creepy when it was woods," said the driver. "I hated it. There was always a lot of people disappearing or having stuff grow on their faces if they slept there. You know, puff balls or stuff. Or another eye. This guy from Dellisburg, he camped here for a week and he got this itch in his cheek, and after a few weeks, he developed another eye. I mean a cheek eye. I hate that stuff. I grew up near here. I was always: 'No way I'm camping there. I already wear glasses. I don't want to have to wear glasses and a monocle, too.'"

"Another *eye*?" said Brian.

36

"Yeah. It saw stuff his normal eyes didn't see. This was back in the day."

"Did you ever actually see this guy?" Gregory asked. "Or is this just hearsay and rumor?"

The driver laughed. "Hearsay and rumor," he said. "What else? Doesn't matter now, anyhow. It's great they have this community here. It really takes away the creepiness."

The wagon soared without sound over the broad, richly laid tarmac.

The driver added, "Except people say the creepiness is coming back."

"Here?" said Brian.

"From the storm drains and stuff. From up on the mountain. Kind of invading the neighborhood. Like they shouldn't have built anything here. Not so fast. Without being careful, you know, of what they disturbed."

"Great," said Gregory.

When they got to Prudence's house, Brian didn't recognize it at first. He remembered it being sunk in the gloom of white-pine woods and dense firs. Now it was surrounded by houses.

Brian looked up and down the street. They might have been put up too quickly, but he was thankful for the new homes. He was kind of scared, and he liked the look of neighbors. People were just getting home from work, turning down their freshly paved driveways and calling hello to each other across their lawns.

"Witnesses," said Gregory.

Brian nodded.

Gregory said, "Much harder for us to be torn apart by ogres if people are playing Wiffle ball in our backyard."

They thanked the driver. Brian calculated the tip. Gregory paid him.

The whole time, they were watching Prudence's house. No sign of motion. No sign anyone had been home for some days. The lawn looked like it hadn't been mowed in a while. There were newsprint circulars stuffed in between the screen door and the front door.

Gregory rang the bell. As they expected, there was no answer.

Then Gregory knocked. They waited.

Up the street, little kids were riding bikes with training wheels. They cheered and spun in circles.

Gregory said, "I don't have a real good feeling about this."

Brian shook his head. "Do you have the key?"

Gregory nodded and took it out of his pocket.

He rang the bell again. They knocked again. Gregory leaned toward the glass panels of the door and shouted, "Prudence? Prudence, it's Gregory."

No answer.

Gregory turned the key in the lock. He opened the door. A foul smell issued out.

Together, they entered the house.

FIVE

The cat box was full. It sat by the front door, the turds old, dry, and frosted white. That explained the smell. Beside it sat the cat's water and food dishes, empty.

Brian and Gregory looked up and down the entry steps. There was no sign of motion. Upstairs, pleasant daylight shone through dirty windows. The place was in a much better state than when Brian had been there the last time, hiding with Kalgrash while a Thusser agent had tracked them through the wood. It had been a ruin then. Now there was a sofa and a few stuffed chairs in the living room. There was a television. A magazine was open on the floor, as if someone had been reading and had just fled from the room.

Gregory pointed up and pointed down with a quizzical look on his face, as if to say, *Which first?*

Brian shrugged. Gregory nodded slightly and walked silently up the four steps that led to the main floor of the house.

The two kept close together. There was nothing else to see in the living room. On the walls, Prudence had hung Norumbegan art — old scrolls, matted and framed, depicting an ancient tale of men in robes and top hats. Above the mantelpiece was a Norumbegan blunderbuss.

They stepped on the carpet like the floor was about to give way at the touch of their toes and buck them into a pit. Brian couldn't help but feel that something was hunched in one of the rooms, spike nosed, half turned from a trail of carnage, listening. Something, he felt, was waiting.

They kept moving through the house.

Nothing in the kitchen to see. Dishes and a frying pan in the sink. A stink from rotting pork. On the refrigerator were sepia photos of Gregory and Brian engaged in the Game, whispering to each other in a gloomy hallway or sitting on a hassock by the fire, looking frightened and guilty.

Carefully pressing his fingers against the handle, Brian swung the fridge open.

Gregory whispered, "Can't the party pizzas wait till later?"

"I'm sniffing the milk," Brian said.

"Sniffing the milk."

Brian nodded. "And stuff. To see if it's rotten." There were several Tupperware containers filled with scraps. All of the scraps and the curdling beans were spotted with mold.

"It's been a while," whispered Brian, grimly.

Gregory opened the cupboard.

40

"What are you looking for?" Brian asked.

"Hidden intruders. Listen: We are looking in every closet. Every single one. Together. And you're pulling back the shower curtain. I am really unhappy."

Brian was really unhappy, too. His stomach was tight. His elbows wanted to jump. He complained, "Why do I have to be the one who pulls back the shower curtain?"

"Your skills."

"Skills."

"Exactly."

"Thanks."

First, they progressed into the master bedroom. Bookshelves, skirts on the floor, a laptop on a desk, a gold-leaf mandala from Nepal hanging above the bed. The bed itself was wrenched apart. The comforter had been yanked to the side. The fitted sheet had popped its corners. The mattress was skewed on the box spring.

"Every closet," said Gregory, pointing at the slats of Prudence's closet door.

They stood to one side of it and Gregory flung it open.

Clothes. A few stuffed animals. Charcoal sketches of tennis shoes and conch shells that Prudence had done in some art class.

Brian inspected Prudence's laptop.

"It's on," he said.

"Sleep mode?"

"Yeah. The light's flashing. Should we check what she was doing?"

"Let's check out the rest of the house first," said Gregory. "To make sure that Gelt the Winnower isn't

41

waiting for us in the bathroom. I don't like this. I'm still unhappy."

"Me too," said Brian.

The bathroom . . . makeup on the counter, smears of flesh-colored powder by the soap . . . nothing in the shower. The dining room . . . a glass table and mismatched chairs . . . a painting of Prudence in one of her nineteenth-century dresses, holding a doll with a spyglass as a head. Otherwise, nothing.

So they went downstairs.

Brian hated it every time they opened a new door. At each one, he tensed and flinched. Gregory opened the closets. Brian stood to the side. Gregory's mouth was fixed in a line. But they found nothing.

Part of the basement was unfinished. It was just concrete floors and metal poles. The furnace. Power tools.

Part was carpeted. A television room. In the television room, there was a door.

Gregory went to open it.

"That's where they found the guy who died," said Brian. "Last time. That guy who went into the woods. Who went crazy. He ran here and hid in that room. He lay there until he starved to death."

Gregory blanched. He took his hand away from the knob.

Brian stepped up and turned it, then walked in.

The room was empty. The walls had been repainted white. There were neat rows of small brass objects on the floor, ordered like ants. They formed a grid.

"What are they?" whispered Gregory.

42

"Norumbegan protective charms," said Brian. "A lot of the books she gave me to read were sealed with them."

Gregory looked around and backed up. "What are they protecting against?"

Brian wrinkled his lips and fiddled with the doorknob. He didn't answer because he didn't know. They left the room and Brian closed the door behind them. "She must not have wanted to use the room again. I don't blame her."

"I don't like that room," said Gregory.

"It used to be Prudence's bedroom, I think."

"I wouldn't sleep in there. You couldn't give me a million dollars."

"A million?"

"All right. You could give me a million."

"Let's . . . let's go back upstairs and check out her laptop."

"You go do that. I want to go and ask those kids outside if they've seen anything," said Gregory. "At least then we'll know exactly how long she's been gone."

They had made it up the stairs as far as the front door. Gregory pulled the door open. "Back in a sec," he said, and walked out.

Brian watched the door swing closed. He didn't want to keep going up the steps. He wished he'd gone with Gregory, or that Gregory had agreed to come along and check the computer. One of the two.

Either way, he was alone now.

He went up the stairs and down the hall to Prudence's room.

The computer blinked softly on the desk.

Brian slid the window open so he could hear Gregory calling out to the circle of little kids. He wanted to be able to shout if anything went wrong.

Brian brushed the mouse to wake the computer from its hibernation.

"Hey," he heard Gregory say. "I'm the cousin of the woman who lives in that house over there. Prudence. Hey there. Hi. Yeah, you, too — hi. Have you seen her around?"

The kids were maybe about seven or eight. They clustered around Gregory.

"She's disappeared," said Gregory. "Did any of you see her leave or see anything unusual?"

"She has donuts," said a boy. "She gave us donuts."

"She had a box," another kid agreed. "She gave us one each."

"Donuts," said Gregory. "When was this?"

The computer, roused, asked Brian if he wanted to resume. He did.

A child said, "Mine was a Boston cream."

"Fascinating," Gregory responded. "This is all great stuff. When did she give you the donuts?"

"A month."

"A month ago?"

The child wouldn't respond, became coy. And then the kids were throwing out times at random: "A week." — "Two. Two whole weeks." — "Are you her dad?"

The screen flashed, and it was back to how it must have been when Prudence last saw it. E-mail. She had been in the middle of writing an e-mail.

44

Brian squinted at the screen.

"Could we settle on just one answer?" Gregory asked his crowd.

Brian felt a chill go down his spine.

It was an e-mail, half written. She had been writing to him and Gregory when she had disappeared.

He bent closer to read it.

SIX

Gregory didn't especially like little kids. He and Brian had suffered through a disastrous summer of babysitting a couple of years before. Mrs. Thatz had told them that it would be a powerful learning experience, and indeed it had been. The most important lessons were about how easy it was to break expensive stereo equipment with ice cream and when to use a tourniquet. It was a summer that Gregory referred to as "Babies Get Rabies."

Now Gregory looked around his circle of admirers. What particularly bothered him was that they looked like they kind of *pitied* him. They were sorry he had apparently lost his cousin and that he seemed kind of irritated by their help. He felt like they were about to offer him more information regarding donuts.

"Okay, my sticky little friends," he concluded. "It's time to question a higher power."

He broke through their ranks and headed for a house

a few doors down, where a mom was climbing out of her SUV.

"Hi there!" he said. "Hey!"

She was tall and pale. She wore slacks that were business casual and carried a stack of color photocopies under her arm. "Hi," she said, without enthusiasm.

"I'm Gregory. I'm Prudence's cousin. She lives in that house there, just past the corner."

"The little sixties one?"

"Yeah. I'm just wondering if you've seen her around."

"Seen her?"

"Recently."

The mom looked vexed. She called her kids. "Cassie. Charlton. Come on." She turned back to Gregory. "I'm worried about her," she admitted. "She's really nice. We met her when we moved in. It looks like things are falling apart over there."

"She's missing, I think. I've come up to look for her."

"We've been worried about her. Her car's in the driveway."

"Do you have any idea where she might be? Or have you seen anything strange going on over there?"

"She's been gone for . . . I don't know . . . three weeks or a month."

"I've heard from her more recently than that."

"Maybe it's been more than a month."

"I got an e-mail from her a couple of weeks ago."

"It seems like a long time," said the woman. Her eyes were on the trees.

"Have you noticed anything?" Gregory asked. "I'm talking *unusual*. Things that skulk or are mysterious."

"Like what?"

"A guy in a hat. Big centipedes. Anything."

"She's not the only one," the woman whispered. "I'm afraid something's going on."

"What?"

"Something's invading."

"What have you seen?"

"The Carruthers are gone."

"I don't know the Carruthers."

"They live on Heather Lane. Everyone knows they're gone."

"Has someone called the police?"

The woman looked at him like he was crazy.

He said, "So the Carruthers and Prudence."

"I think there are others," the woman said. "I think people are disappearing."

Gregory stepped back from the woman. She kneaded the keys in her hands. Her car key scraped back and forth on the ring. "Then we've all got to do something," said Gregory.

"We've got to stay happy," the woman replied. She did not seem to be speaking to him.

Gregory looked at her in perplexity. "How long have you lived here?" he asked.

She looked startled. "Six months," she answered. "About six months. I completely forgot my groceries. I think I left them at the store. You know how you sometimes do that?"

"Sure," said Gregory, who had never left his groceries at the store.

"I guess I've got to drive back and get them. Cassie! Charlton! Come over here and get in the car."

They arrived, looking, to Gregory's eye, dazed. "He's the donut lady's cousin," said Charlton, crawling up into the backseat. Cassie clambered up after him.

"Okay," said the woman. She nodded faintly, as if Gregory were a spirit who had just given her instructions and faded. She got back into her car and shut the door.

"Thank you!" said Gregory, trying to put on his most amiable, adult-pleasing smile.

She didn't notice him. She almost backed out over him.

She drove off slowly.

Watching her car roll down the smooth lane, he shook his head.

He walked back to Prudence's house to see if Brian had found anything.

SEVEN

Brian rose from the office chair to let Gregory have a seat and read the e-mail. Gregory rolled the chair to the desk. He swiveled from side to side. "What's it say?" he asked Brian.

"Read it for yourself," Brian said.

Gregory scrolled down the page.

It was from Prudence to the two of them. Their addresses were already in the *To:* field. She'd never had a chance to send it. She had written:

B and G —

Something is going wrong. Wee Snig is missing. Just hiked up to find him and he's gone. I'm worried something is watching me. I don't know if it's the Thusser. Why would they bother?

I'd say come up and we'll investigate, but I don't think you should. It's not safe. The neighborhood is getting dangerous. I think I've been confused. We're all confused.

50

I don't know what to do. I'm coming down to Boston tomorrow. I have to clear my head. G, tell your parents I want to crash in the guest room. Remember: No rayon sheets.

I'm afraid for tonight. I think they might try to grab me. Whoever they are.

If they try anything, they'll have to deal with my old friend Bess. If they so much as knock on my front door, I'll say the magic word to her and they'll be sorry.

I really do hope that

"That's it," said Brian. "As if she was typing, when she suddenly heard something and got up."

"Or got grabbed," murmured Gregory. He looked sick. "Too bad it's not dated."

"She would've had to have sent it for it to have a date," said Brian.

"Yeah," said Gregory. "Let's get out of this house."

"We have to keep looking for clues," said Brian.

"We can walk around the neighborhood," Gregory said. "Things are going on. Other people have disappeared. The Carruthers. Over on Heather Lane."

"The Carruthers?"

"Nice people. Super-nice people. Great at a barbecue. Vamoosed."

"How do you know?"

"Lady down at Number Four Fisher Way told me."

"Okay," said Brian. "Let's look around." An idea suddenly struck him. "Let's find Kalgrash. We can sleep at his place."

51

Gregory seemed to relax. "That's a great idea. That is so much better than sleeping here and waiting for something with more eyes than legs to come crawling up from the basement."

The two set out, locking the door behind them.

The circle of kids wheeled slowly at the intersection, chirping to one another in the summer sunlight.

"Hey there," said Gregory. "Hi. Hey. Yo. Munchkin brigade."

"You find that lady yet?"

"My cousin? No. We're still looking. Here's another question: Do you know what happened to her cat?"

"Melior," said a little girl. "She's really cute."

"She's the cutest," said another.

A third said, "I — when she was gone, Prudence, when she was gone to Boston a couple months ago — I watched Melior for her. I let myself in with the key and I fed her. If you pat her just by her tail, kind of thumpy, if you pat her there? She licks the carpet."

"Yeah," said Gregory. "That's Prudence for you."

"No. The cat. Melior. If you thump her side near her tail, she —"

"I know. Joke. Have you seen Melior recently?"

"She's the cutest," said one of the girls.

"I haven'en't seen her for six years," claimed a boy who was maybe five.

"All right," Gregory said to Brian. "I'm done. So much for the caramel parade. Let's go."

"Thank you!" said Brian to the kids, waving, because Gregory clearly wasn't going to thank anyone, and Brian thought kids deserved to be thanked. He wished, frankly, that he could spend the evening playing on lawns and riding bikes, like he and Gregory used to do when they were seven and it was summer and night fell late.

The kids all stared while the two boys walked away.

When Brian and Gregory had followed the soft curve of the road and were finally out of sight, the children began to revolve in circles again, cooing to each other like doves.

EIGHT

S treet led to street. The day was bright, and the grass shone beneath the sprinklers as if gemmed. Behind the houses there were small stands of white pine marking off individual yards. Brian and Gregory walked along, watching carefully for any detail that might suggest danger. It was almost six, and more parents were getting home from work. Their wheels hushed past on the tarmac.

Everything was peaceful.

Brian didn't like the peace. Something was coming, he felt instinctively — something that hated the slumber and ease of this community. They had built their suburb over something ancient and dangerous, and whatever lived beyond the rim of the world and peered through into this one would now exact revenge. It didn't matter that the houses looked firm and complacent on their lawns. There was something in the mountains that wanted it all to blacken and burn at the edges, that wanted to crawl forth, astonish, and destroy.

The adhesive golden numbers on mailboxes were still new, and sparkled in the light.

At the corner of Fisk and Yastrzemski there was a green electrical box surrounded by a moat of red wood chips. Though there was a sticker on the side saying DANGER and PELIGRO, with a stick figure getting shocked, three ten-year-old girls were sitting on top of the box, staring up at the mountain. One sometimes spun a soccer ball on her finger.

"Excuse me," said Brian to the ten-year-olds. "Do you know where Heather Lane is?"

Gregory added, "The Carruthers's."

The three girls turned their gaze on the boys. One chewed a piece of gum a few times. They didn't answer. They just stared.

"That's great. Thanks," said Gregory. "Your check is in the mail."

One of them gestured with her shoulder. "Down there," she said. "Toward the middle." She had a Southern accent. "That's where Heather Lane is. I think."

Another girl said, "We don't go down there."

"This is our street."

"We stay on this street."

"Do you know any Carruthers?" Gregory asked.

The one with gum chewed it.

"The middle of what?" Brian asked.

"What does he mean, the middle of what?" the girl with the Southern accent asked Gregory.

The fair-haired boy explained, "You said Heather Lane was near the middle. Of what?"

"This," said the girl. Her friend or sister whirled the ball. It didn't stay aloft for long.

"What about a river?" Brian asked. "Is there a river around here anywhere?"

"River?" one asked another. "What are they talking about, with a river?"

"There's a river. Down there." The girl with the ball pointed. "I guess you think we shouldn't be sitting on this box."

"No," said Brian. "I mean . . . no, I don't."

"In fact, I was hoping you'd crawl inside it," said Gregory, smiling. "All three of you."

One of the girls gave a grunt of irritation and flopped on her back. The electrical box gave a tinny thump and dust drifted out its gills.

"Thank you," said Brian, waving. "Thanks!"

None of the girls moved. The ball spun on one unmoving finger.

Brian and Gregory walked on.

"That was friendly," said Gregory. He tapped his fingers on mailboxes they passed, as if playing Duck, Duck, Goose. "They were kind of young to be that sarcastic. Don't you think people should wait for sarcasm? Like learning to eat oysters."

"Oysters?" said Brian.

"Do you like oysters?"

"No."

"I didn't think so," said Gregory, as if that proved something.

They followed the girl's vague description to get to

56

the river. It was only a couple of blocks before they found it. What had been the River of Time and Shadow now crossed under the road in an aluminum culvert. The grass in the yards around it looked thin and nude. Almost all of the trees that had once overarched the river had been cut down. A clump of hemlocks still stood on one bank. A few awkward aspens, trembling with exposure, gawked by the river's shore at new mansions. Behind them rose the mountain, dark and solemn.

"There it is," said Gregory. "The River of Time and Shadow. Do you recognize where we are? How far along we are?"

Brian shook his head, sucking at his lips.

"Which way do you think Kalgrash's bridge is?"

Brian walked to the edge of the road and squinted down the meanders of the brook. He shrugged.

Gregory asked, "What do you want to do?"

"I think we should follow it this way," said Brian. "It looks less built up down there."

Gregory nodded and they climbed down the bank. They walked along the side of the river.

Brian mused, "Who do you think 'Bess' is?"

"Who?"

"Bess. In her e-mail, Prudence said that her old friend Bess would protect her."

"I've never heard her talk about anyone named Bess before," Gregory considered.

"Yeah. I don't think it's a person. I just get this feeling that Bess is an object of some kind."

"An object?"

"Something." Brian shrugged. "I think she was joking. Boasting." He looked around. "Are we going through people's yards?"

"Yeah," said Gregory. "See? Grills aren't naturally occurring."

Brian stopped.

"What's wrong?" asked Gregory.

"We shouldn't go through people's yards."

"What's the problem?"

"It's private property."

"We're saving them from certain death. Or disappearance."

"What if someone gets angry?"

"We'll bake them a cherry pie. We'll kiss them on the nose." Gregory yanked his friend by the wrist and, when Brian had stumbled past him, kneed him in the butt.

"*Ow*," said Brian. "It's weird how hard it is to remember what the woods looked like before these houses were built."

Gregory squinted along the river. "I know. It's like the forest was never here. One of the strange things about suburbia. It always seems like it belongs. I can't hardly even picture the forest anymore."

"Yeah! That's what I mean exactly," said Brian. "But if you . . ." He didn't finish his sentence.

They had come upon a soccer field beside the river. There was a game going on. Cars were lined up by the side of the field, and parents were gossiping by the sidelines. Kids bopped a ball back and forth across the halfway line.

Brian had stopped, stock-still.

"What's up?" said Gregory. "Oh, the beauty of the game. Yup." He nodded appreciatively. "Whoa. That kid totally should have gotten a yellow card for shin kicking."

"No," Brian whispered. "Get down." He crouched on his knees, surrounded by rushes.

"What's going on?"

"The guy who followed me in Boston is there. He's watching the game."

"You're kidding."

"No. With the reddish face and the pink polo shirt."

"And chinos?"

"Yeah."

"You wouldn't think that evil from beyond time would wear chinos." Gregory ducked down next to Brian. "Then again, you wouldn't think that evil from beyond time would be a big follower of little league soccer."

"Gregory, what are we going to do?"

"I think it's just great he shows an interest."

"Do you think he saw us?"

"He's pretty much facing the other way."

"We can't go back the way we came. He'll see us for sure when we pass. We have to go this way, but with our faces turned as much to the other side of the river as possible."

"All right."

Brian demanded, "Face over there when you stand up. And don't look back."

"*Ja*, Herr Kommandant."

"It's not funny."

59

"I'm not laughing."

They rose, facing the opposite bank, and walked carefully along the river's edge, leaving the parents' shouts behind them. They could practically feel the peering of the eyes in that ripple-skinned face.

All he would see, Brian figured, was two boys walking by the river. Nothing unusual in that. Kicking along, thinking about swimming maybe, picking up old packaging wedged in the dirt.

They couldn't tell if he ever turned and looked at them directly. They didn't want to check.

In a couple of minutes, a few willows that had been left to shelter the bank were hanging between them and the game. A few minutes after that, the river was squelching through a construction site, huge tire tracks gouged in the wet earth, rushes growing in mud, the water all brown and red where it had gone stagnant. New houses were going up. Frames already stood amid mounds of dirt and rock. Some walls were sheeted in Tyvek.

"I wonder where this was," said Brian. "When it was woods. It could have been anywhere. Kalgrash's cave could have been right here."

"There was more rock, wasn't there? Where he was?"

Brian pointed at the huge boulders that had been yanked up and stacked.

They heard footsteps approaching them at a run, splattering through the puddles.

Brian darted for cover. Gregory followed.

They hung close to the mounds. Brian leaned forward

so far that he pressed his fingers into the wall of earth to hold himself. It was unclear where the footsteps were coming from.

Gregory exhaled in surprise. There was a man.

He was jogging through the construction. He wore shorts, and his armpits were ringed with sweat.

"Hey," he said, and jogged in place.

"Hi there," said Gregory.

"You kids know to go home before dark, don't you?" the man said. "You shouldn't be hanging out here. The curfew."

"What's the curfew?" said Gregory.

"It's not official," said the jogger.

Brian asked carefully, "When should we be home?"

"Gets dark at, what, eight o'clock or something? You have a half an hour. I'm just saying."

"Yup," said Gregory.

"Last week, there was a chariot."

"Was there?" Gregory asked.

"Don't you guys ever look out windows? There's a car, but pulled by horses." The man kept running in place while he lifted up the belly of his shirt and wiped his face. He said, "It looked weird and dead. Oh, and don't forget: There's Gelt the Winnower."

Brian started. "How did you hear about Gelt the Winnower?"

"He patrols the streets sometimes at night. Guy with lots of wires coming out of him." The man shook his head. "The neighborhood association told us to stay inside."

Brian and Gregory exchanged a look.

Brian said, "Are you okay with that? Living with . . . Gelt . . . and chariots?"

"You got to put up with some stuff," the man said. "But you should get inside by dark. 'Kay, pal?"

" 'Kay," said Gregory.

The man jogged away through the torn landscape.

Brian and Gregory made their way back to the paved road.

"Gelt," said Brian, uneasily.

"I know. Gelt."

"Something's being done by whatever's invading," said Brian, "so that people in the suburb don't know what's hit them. They're not afraid enough. Prudence talked about being 'confused.' I think this is what she meant."

"They can't think straight."

"Everyone seems a little hypnotized."

"It *is* surburbia."

"Eight o'clock," said Brian. He looked at his watch. "We've got to be home by then. Hey, what time do you have?"

"None o'clock. I don't have a watch."

Brian took out his phone. It didn't get reception, but the clock still worked. He insisted, "Gregory, check the time on your phone."

"Oh, sure." Gregory looked and said, "Six twenty."

"My watch says three thirty," said Brian, "and my phone says it's almost eight."

"Let's believe your watch. Then we can sleep in."

"It's strange that . . ." Brian was looking across the

road at an office and a model home. He picked up speed and started to run.

Gregory squawked, "What? What's —?" and ran after him.

When Gregory caught up, Brian was standing, looking at a huge sign hung in front of the office.

Gregory asked, "What's up?"

Brian pointed at the sign. It showed an elk poised — with a hoof raised and with the sun glinting on its antlers — on a rock in front of someone's driveway. In the background, kids played amid the firs.

"What?" said Gregory. "It's an elk coming home from work."

"Read it."

"An elk can take pride in its home, Brian. An elk can enjoy a carpeted rec room as much as the next man."

"Gregory!" snapped Brian.

Gregory smirked and turned to read the sign. It said:

Rumbling Elk Haven
LUXURY RESIDENTIAL COMMUNITY

"Come Join the Dream"

NEW CONSTRUCTION
LOTS FROM .5 — 2 ACRES
FEATURING SIX UNIQUE HOME DESIGNS
FROM 2,500 — 3,500 SQ. FT.
INQUIRIES: MILTON DEATLEY,
SALES AND FINANCING OFFICE
RUMBLING ELK HAVEN

"So what?" said Gregory. "They sure got to work fast, but still."

"See who's in charge of it?"

"Milton Deatley," Gregory read out. "Inquiries."

"Milton Deatley," Brian insisted.

"Uh-huh?"

Brian whispered, voice tight with fear, "Milton Deatley died a year ago of starvation and insanity in Prudence's basement."

NINE

Prudence was a terrible housekeeper. As they cooked dinner — pizzas from the freezer, the only unspoiled food in the house — they discovered that everything in the kitchen was covered in gray cat hair. It was stuck to the sides of the counters, mired in grease and scumming up the sink. Brian ran a paper towel around the stove top; after one circuit, it came away shaggy.

"It's like she cooked the cat," he said, disgusted. He threw the hairy towel away.

"Look at you, cleaning," said Gregory. "We should just put you in a calico apron."

Brian gave him a dark look and kept swiping at the burners.

They felt strangely adult to be cooking their own dinner. It would have been kind of fun — choosing movies to watch, hanging out — if there hadn't been an undercurrent of unease and terror.

The pizzas took forty-five minutes to cook. The boys were starving by the time the food was ready. They sat down at the dining room table, the computer in front of them, and got to work.

"I'm sure Milton Deatley is the name of the guy who died," said Brian. "We're going to search the newspaper archives for him. There'll be an obituary or something."

"There's even hair on the glass table," said Gregory. "How can glass be hairy?"

Brian went to the local paper's web page. He typed in *Milton Deatley* and did a search. "Several hits," he said.

The first was a real estate listing from a few days before. "'Rumbling Elk Haven,'" Brian read. "'Luxury Homes. Why rent when you can own?'" He scrolled down. "'Call Milton Deatley. . . .'"

"He clearly still thinks he's alive," said Gregory.

"There are some more real estate listings here. Going back . . . only a month." Brian frowned. "This neighborhood must have been here longer than a month."

"It's huge."

"Yeah. But there aren't any more hits for a while before that. Back until . . . okay, in January, he appeared at a town meeting . . . to get some kind of zoning permission."

"What's a zoning permission?"

"To be allowed to build. It says here he was trying to get permission to build on twenty 'percable lots.'"

"Twenty? We saw like a million and fifty." Gregory sawed his pizza into patchwork. "I guess we don't know whether they were 'percable,' though. Did you notice any 'percing'?"

"Let's go back further," said Brian. "Next page."

66

The next hit was a longer article. He gaped at it silently. Gregory worked industriously at his pizza, popping cheesy little trapezoids into his mouth and wiping his hands on paper towels.

"Read this," said Brian, sliding the computer over to Gregory.

"I'm really greasy," said Gregory. "Can you do the mouse?"

"Just wipe off your hands."

"There's nothing that can absorb this much grease. I'd need a yak."

"Gregory," Brian said, irritably. "This is big."

Gregory nodded and read.

LOCAL MAN DECLARED MISSING

Gerenford, VT., June 7 — Gerenford police have declared local man Milton Deatley missing in the Norumbega Wood. His car was found by the edge of the forest four days ago.

Deatley, 37, a real estate developer responsible for Burnside Lane Estates and the Plainfield Stonery, was last seen on June 2 by his secretary, Denise Robbins. "He didn't seem like he was going camping," she says. "He didn't have the right pants."

A search will begin

"Blah, blah, blah," said Gregory.

"No," said Brian. "Then the next one."

REMAINS OF LOCAL MAN FOUND IN NORUMBEGA WOOD

Gerenford, VT., June 15 — Missing real estate developer Milton Deatley, 43, was declared dead today after his remains were discovered in an abandoned house on Howard Road. The body was badly mauled by wild animals. Police say it will likely be impossible to determine the cause of death.

Deatley was first declared missing one week ago, on June 7. His car was found abandoned at the edge of the Norumbega Wood on June 3.

"When we heard he hadn't shown up to work," said Gerenford Police Chief Donald DeVries, "and we knew his car had been abandoned, we began to suspect the worst."

There are currently no leads in the mysterious death. "It is very hard to determine what happened to Mr. Deatley," said Chief DeVries. "He may have died of natural causes, but then some animals got to him. There just isn't much left of the body. Not enough to make a meal. Only a couple of pounds of bone and some hair. No one could eat that. You couldn't put tongue to teeth and swallow it. We become, eventually, inedible. But sadly, that's all that remains. You live a bunch of years, and then what is left is too little to serve a full supper to ghouls."

Deatley himself says, "I have returned. In the night, I heard the owl sing. Now my britches are stitched up and I extend my hands in all directions. Have you seen what passes beneath the mountain? It can

"Whoa, whoa, whoa!" exclaimed Gregory. "What? Huh?"

"Exactly," said Brian. "Something's happened to the article. And notice his age. He's thirty-seven in the first article and forty-three in the second one."

"The years really fly by."

"What do you think it means?" Brian asked, tense.

Gregory reread the end of the article.

"It is very hard to determine what happened to Mr. Deatley," said Chief DeVries. "He may have died of natural causes, but then some animals got to him. There just isn't much left of the body. Just bone and hair. It will make the autopsy difficult."

"He is gone," DeVries explains, "though he may return. But we are all animals, all the heirs of bone and hair, and we should all sing beneath the moon in our pack to lament the passing of Deatley the burrow maker, the mound builder, this lone man in the wood, this Lord of Cat and Asplundh."

"This is incredible," said Gregory. "It's different already."

"Let me see," said Brian, sliding the laptop over toward him.

"Grabby," said Gregory.

"'He may have died of natural causes,'" Brian read, "'but then some animals got to him. He died, hunted and alone. He fled in fear. He hid in madness. He collapsed in need. When he was gone, he —'"

69

"We can't even read the real article," said Gregory. "It's being blocked somehow. And changed."

Brian stared, amazed, at the screen. "Somehow," he said, "no one in town realizes that they're buying houses from a dead man."

"He must be pretty charming," Gregory guessed. "The gift of gab. You know salesmen."

Brian gaped. "Look at the newspaper's main page. Look at it. Check out the date."

Gregory looked at it. "Are you sure this is the main page?" he asked.

"Yeah," said Brian. "And it says it's a month from now."

They started examining the page closely. Everywhere they looked, there were small errors and replacements. More and more words were spelled wrong. Then Gregory's eye was caught by an ad — a line drawing of a man in a blazer and slacks — a sale at some tiny clothing store. The man had three arms.

Other ads were for incomprehensible items — iron heaven, soul brittle, bombast spheres, or lymph.

They could not keep their eyes on the screen. It flickered with change.

"Something's happening here," Brian whispered. "Something's happening to time. And lots of other things. Time is shifting. Or warping." He looked at his watch, and said, "Twelve thirty." He scrounged in his pocket and pulled out his phone. He flipped it open and looked at the screen. "Nine twenty. What's your phone say?"

"Just after eight," said Gregory.

"Time is all wrong. That's why no one says the same thing when we ask them when Prudence disappeared. And that's . . ."

"I know what you're going to say."

"Gregory, that's how all these houses were built so quickly. Time is running differently. Remember the clock that used to be in the forest, telling time for other worlds? That's what's happening now. Time here is moving like we're in another world."

Gregory swore softly.

Now that Brian had said it, they both could almost feel it, something slipping across their skin, something robbing minutes or slowing them to a crawl — time as breathable as air and thick as smoke.

Brian flipped his phone closed. "No signal," he said. "Try yours. Call your parents. We need to check the date."

Gregory dialed. "No signal," he said.

Brian was pale. Gregory looked panicked. Brian stood up and started to walk toward the living room, then turned back. He didn't know where to go, what to say.

"Gregory," he said, "there isn't an ancient evil invading the neighborhood."

"Huh?" said Gregory. "What are you suggesting? The Girl Scouts?"

"No, what I mean is, this isn't a situation where the development was built on top of something magical that's trying to get out." Brian sat down. He stared through the glass table at his knees. He couldn't sit still. He stood up.

71

He said, "The development itself is the invasion. Somehow, Milton Deatley, this dead developer, is bringing something into this world. The houses, the time jumble, everything. I don't know why, but he's bringing it here, and we're all trapped in it. And tomorrow — tomorrow we're going to go to his office and find out what he's planning."

Outside, at the crossroads, in the dark, the kids rode their bicycles in circles. There were rectangles of light across the lawns and through the bushes and trees. They were lights from kitchens with granite countertops, from dens and marble-floored foyers. The children did not pay attention to their homes. They rode their bikes in circles. Some cried because they were so tired, but still they wheeled and spun as the night drew on and the crickets began to sing of heat and shadow.

TEN

Evidently, the cat usually slept next to Prudence's head. Her pillow was shaggy. Brian choked on gray fur. Gregory was sleeping on the floor. They wouldn't go into separate rooms. It was a hot night, so the window was open. Soft, small things nuzzled against the screen.

There was a light on in the room. Prudence had a Norumbegan lantern hung above the bed. Before they went to bed, Brian had lit it with the Cantrip of Activation.

Watching him use this paltry spell, Gregory had said, "See, the problem with me trying to cast the Cantrip is that when you say not to think about other things — like don't think about school — that's exactly what I think about. I'm thinking, *I wonder if it counts as thinking about school yet, if I'm just thinking about thinking about school*. And then the spell doesn't work."

"We can try again. Just . . . you can't get angry at me."

"I'm just saying I'd like to know something about magic. This is getting crazy and dangerous. It's not fair

73

that you can walk around knowing some magic and I don't know anything. It's got nothing to do with who won the Game. Just because you won the Game doesn't mean that you're Einstein."

"I know."

"Because I could have won the Game. It could have been me."

Brian didn't want to argue. Even this much argument made him nervous. So he agreed to try to teach Gregory the Cantrip of Activation again, maybe in the morning, and they both went to bed.

As Brian lay in Prudence's bed, he got angrier and angrier that Gregory had said he could just as easily have won the Game. Brian felt like he had deserved it. He had noticed all kinds of things that Gregory hadn't. He had been the one who'd realized that they were playing for different teams. He'd been the one in the greatest danger. And even as he lay there, filled with petty anger, Brian was haunted by images of what might still lurk on the streets and in the dark corners behind houses.

He stared at the mandala hanging above him. The power switch from Prudence's slumbering laptop pulsed blue as if in dreamy respiration. Brian thought about her fingers hanging above that white keyboard, her thumb bumping the space bar just before she — what? Was whisked away or bludgeoned from behind? He cringed. The thought of something stalking toward her on the carpet — or she was gagged or called distantly to the door by something with the voice of a neighbor or a high school friend but the hands of a maniac — some crisis . . . and now where was she? He was paralyzed by the possibilities: some cell, some alien labyrinth, or hunted, panting, through boulders and up mountain slopes. Even right now, this moment, in the dark, hoping that someone was thinking of her, tracing clues — but all the while, fearing some claw, some hook, some sword.

Brian could not sleep at first, and when sleep came, his dreams were of circular roads, patios, rising lawns under which their owners slept, girls crawling through new basements. He dreamed of a spire of stone, and then grids — hours of grids — wiring, plumbing, hands reaching through pipes.

He was awakened by hooves.

Brian sat up. His hair was in his eyes, and so was the cat's. He didn't have his glasses on. Something murky was happening on the street, and Gregory was half up, already tense with alarm.

"What is it?" Brian whispered.

Gregory rose, crouched, and went to the window. He said nothing. There were enough hoof falls for a team of horses. Their rhythm was slow and leisurely.

Brian found his glasses and made it to Gregory's side.

First he saw that the children were still wheeling in their circles, now silent, faces blank, riding at the crossroads.

"What are they — ?" he began, and then stopped.

Coming up the street was an old black car, chrome shining, drawn by four white horses.

The boys had seen it once before in this forest. It had been driven by the Thusser.

75

Now it was led by a small procession of figures in armor, spiked and fierce, all carrying torches. Behind it, something danced.

Brian was gone from the window and stumbling for the door.

"You can't go out there!" Gregory hissed. "Stop!"

Brian didn't answer. Gregory ran after him and, in the hallway, grabbed his arm. "It's dangerous!"

"What about those kids?" Brian asked furiously.

"Would you think for a minute?" said Gregory.

"Let me go! They're in danger!"

"There's nothing we can do!"

"We've got to try something! They're right in the way of that procession!"

"Don't be stupid!"

"Let go!"

"I'm supposed to be the stupid one, remember?"

Brian was tired of him saying this. "You're not stupid! Now let me go!" Brian yanked his arm away and bolted down the hall. Soon enough, Gregory heard him thumping down the steps to the front door.

"We can't do anything anyways!" Gregory called after him, but still ran for the stairs.

Brian was sprinting across the unruly yard. He still wore the T-shirt and boxers he'd been sleeping in. He had nothing with which to protect himself.

But the danger appeared, for a second, to have passed.

The kids were motionless, divided into two groups standing at attention. The black car rolled between them.

There was a figure moving behind the windows — a mottled, red hand.

Brian stopped on the edge of the lawn. He could feel himself surveyed. The horses were clopping past, their hoofs loud on the new pavement. The armored soldiers with their torches were already down the street.

The creature that danced and cavorted behind the car was made of some rippling, striated stuff, musculature like glass and gray tar. It had a wide grin and thin eyes. It hopped from leg to leg, swung its arms around, rasped deep in its alien throat. It ducked its head lower than its knees, rose up, and twirled. It landed with the lightness of bricks.

Abruptly, it stopped dancing. It stared from face to face in the little crowd of children.

It wants something, Brian thought.

It held out its hands and walked toward a boy of five or six.

The child was terrified, but did not move.

Brian ran out into the street, screaming.

"Idiot," muttered Gregory, picking up a rake as he plunged across the lawn.

The monster turned to watch Brian approach. It smiled at him kindly. Then it turned back to the little boy and began to lift him off the ground.

The automobile had stopped. Its door swung open.

Brian got to the monster and began punching. He yelled, "Put him down!" and slugged with all his might.

His fist landed with a clunk and a squish.

Shocked, Brian staggered backward. He looked at the monster's flesh. It was boiling in a huge, metallic welt.

The monster set the child down. It turned to Brian, brows creased.

Brian hit it again, and grabbed at his own hand in pain. The beast's flesh looked liquid, but punching it was like smacking solid concrete.

The monster reached out and took Brian's arm. It began to drag him toward the car. Brian's bare feet skipped helplessly across the pavement.

Gregory slammed the haft of the rake into the monster's arm. The flesh gathered where he struck. He hit it again. The monster turned and regarded him dispassionately. Its skin moved as Gregory struck it.

The monster began walking again toward the car's open door.

Gregory tagged along, slamming the rake against the thing, trying to bruise it — scratch it — anything to get it to release Brian. Where he smacked, the skin bunched and calcified.

"I can't hurt it!" said Gregory.

The monster watched each blow fall, and willed its flesh to harden. Each time there was an impact, the meat made a callous there as stiff as stone.

The head of the rake snapped off.

The thing was tired of being smacked by Gregory. It dropped Brian's arm. It confronted his friend.

The blond-haired boy swung the broken rake handle. The beast watched the strike land and smiled at the crack of wood against its gathered, lumpy flesh. After the blow,

78

the skin stayed briefly puckered in a welt, then flowed back to its former ductility.

"There's no way to hurt it!" Gregory cried, slashing out wildly with the wooden handle.

The monster snorted.

Suddenly, Gregory saw Brian pick up a trike and point meaningfully to his own neck.

The monster lunged for Gregory, swiping its crystal paws. Gregory didn't know what Brian meant — but aimed to stab the creature's neck. The spiked end of his stick struck the throat — which hardened — and snapped again — now no use. Gregory screamed as the hard hands grabbed him. The thing moved stiffly, its neck momentarily too encrusted, too calcified to budge.

And at that moment — when it couldn't move its head and couldn't see what was coming — Brian, behind it, walloped it with a tricycle.

The flesh was unprotected, unhardened. The trike sunk, splattered skin, and spewed dark chips. The monster yelped and bucked. It fell, broken, to the street. Its back was in pieces. It oozed black jelly.

The two boys stood, panting, panicked, in the road.

From the automobile came the sound of clapping.

A voice from inside rang out. "Well done, boys. We'll see you soon."

The door slammed shut. The horses lowered their heads and began to drag again. The car rolled forward. The torches processed. The children stared.

The car disappeared around the corner.

The monster lay, shattered, on the street.

79

✳ ✳ ✳

Brian and Gregory spent the next fifteen minutes getting the kids to their houses. They all lived on that street, but it took them a while to wake up from their trance enough — through shaking, through water from a hose — to tell Brian and Gregory who lived where.

When the parents opened the doors to receive each kid, they scolded them as if it were only a late night out. "Where were you? You were supposed to be in by seven thirty — Thank these boys for bringing you home. Thank them!"

One by one, the children went inside. Their bikes were left on their drives.

Cassie and Charlton's mother, Mrs. Drake, recognized Gregory. "Oh, thank you," she said. "Usually they're not out so late." She was half covered in dirt, as if she'd been lying in it. It stained her chin and her pantsuit. She didn't seem to mind, however. She told the kids to get ready for bed.

"You have to keep them inside, ma'am," said Brian. "It's really dangerous out there. Did you see the car? Hooked up to the horses?"

"People speed," said the woman, pressing down her mud-spattered hair. "They go so fast. Where are they trying to get to? Or what are they trying to get away from? Sometimes I wonder."

Brian looked at her oddly. He said, "Mrs. Drake, did you fall down?"

She raised her eyebrow. "What are you suggesting?" She smiled tightly. "Anyway, thank you for sending the kids in. I hope you had a good time playing."

And then she closed the door.

✳ ✳ ✳

By three in the morning, the neighborhood was silent and mostly dark. No one stirred on the streets and culs-de-sac, the lanes and ways, except one child walking in desolate circles, his bike confiscated, his eyes half closed. In the houses, people lay in their beds, some asleep, dreaming of jobs, others staring at the closet door or the blinking of the time. Dogs sighed at the foot of quilts. The mountain rose above them all.

In one house, a boy was awake and pacing. Brian could not sleep. He was too worried. He felt invasion in his chest, the stealthy disruption of rest by anxieties. His unease was physical, and kept him roaming about the living room and kitchen. His hands ached from where he'd hit the solidifying monster. His knuckles were bruised. He couldn't believe that his best friend could sleep at a time like this.

At five, he sat down on the sofa to rest for a minute. He stared at the scrolls framed on the wall. They made no sense, a cavalcade of men in hats. He stared at them until his eyes closed. He tilted his head backward, and at last, was asleep.

In nearby houses, men and women prepared for work.

ELEVEN

The scud of running shoes on pavement woke Gregory up. It was seven thirty — or at least the clock said it was — and a jogger was going past. It was the same man they'd met the day before in the construction zone, who'd told them about the chariot.

Gregory looked around the room. He wished Prudence were there. For one thing, she would have fixed them breakfast. For another, it would have been fun to tell her about the night before. She would have been proud of him, walloping the monster with a rake. *Brave*, she might have called him.

Gregory found Brian asleep in the living room. "Hey, Slumberina."

Brian stirred and looked around, reaching clumsily for his glasses.

"If you weren't going to sleep in the bed," Gregory said, "why didn't you let me use it? The floor was completely uncomfortable."

"Sorry. I couldn't sleep. I came out here."

"I see that."

They ate stale cereal without milk. They didn't speak while they ate. They just pulled cat hair out of their mouths.

They left the house about fifteen minutes later. People were just setting off for their jobs.

"So we're going back to the sales office," said Gregory.

"To meet Milton Deatley," Brian agreed.

"Deceased."

Brian nodded.

Mrs. Drake, no longer dirt covered, was talking to a girl who was about Brian and Gregory's age. "Don't let them watch too much TV," she said. "Unless they're watching those 'Little Achiever' videos. Send them outside to play. There's a lot of kids their age in the neighborhood." She saw Brian and Gregory and waved. "Hi, boys!" she said. "Thanks again for bringing the kids home last night!"

"No problem," said Gregory.

Brian went over to her. "Um, ma'am," he said. "You might want to, you know, keep them with you. More. It really isn't very safe around here. I don't think people understand what's going on."

"What do you mean?"

The babysitter girl was goggling at Brian.

Brian shrugged nervously. "I think that this isn't a normal development. I think there's something wrong here. Someone is watching you and is confusing all of us about time and . . ." He didn't really know how to explain it. The mother was looking at him without any expression.

"You're kind of a creepy boy," she concluded. "Why are you trying to frighten us?"

"I'm not — it's because . . . we have to worry about the, you know, the . . . didn't you see that procession last night?"

"Thanks, anyway, for bringing the kids home," said the woman. "Have a good day."

"I'm not trying to be creepy," said Brian. "But everyone here is in danger."

"From what?"

"From . . . things from outside the world."

"Outside the world," said Mrs. Drake. She looked at the babysitter girl. The babysitter girl was scratching her cheek a lot.

Gregory came up and seized Brian's shoulder. "Ignore him," said Gregory. "This young man's impressionable brain has been fried by rock music, video games, and artificial sweeteners. He's the problem with society today."

"Gregory —" Brian protested.

"Let's go," said Gregory. He apologized to Mrs. Drake. She glared at them and nodded. "I have to get to work," she said.

"See?" said Brian. "That's what I mean about us all being confused. It's Saturday."

"It's not Saturday," said the woman.

"Yesterday was Friday," Brian insisted.

"Maybe she has to work on Saturday," said Gregory.

"It's not Saturday," the woman said. "It's Tuesday."

The babysitter girl looked bored and toed the flowers.

84

"Never mind him," said Gregory. "Sorry. We're sorry." He dragged Brian off.

They kept going down the road.

"Why did you pull me away?" said Brian. "You heard that. She's confused. We're in some kind of time . . . thing. She needs to know. Everyone here needs to know."

"You're not going to convince them by telling them crazy stories about things from other worlds."

"But that's the *truth*."

"What is it with you and the truth? It's not going to get you anywhere."

"How can you say that?"

"They're not going to listen to you. People can only hear what they want to hear."

"Someone's got to tell them how much danger they're in."

"How much danger are they in?"

Brian scowled. "I don't know."

"See?"

"Here's what I think," said Brian. "The Game is being played as a way of settling who owns this territory, right?"

"Right."

"Gregory, I think that the Thusser have given up on the Game. They're ignoring the Rules. They're just taking the territory. This is some kind of first wave of settlement."

"So these are Thusser in the houses?"

"No," said Brian, uneasily. "No, they're people in the houses, but —"

"So your theory doesn't really make sense."

"Right now," said Brian. "But I'm sure that I'll figure something out."

Brian's "I" bugged Gregory. "Oh, you will? Okay," he said, somewhat harshly, "I hope you have something figured out by the time we walk into the sales office and meet the undead guy in charge of this whole outfit. Because I have to admit that I'm starting to wonder why we're going to see him without any way to protect ourselves."

"Someone has to do something," said Brian, "and we know what's going on. We've played the Game."

"And you're the one who gets to design the whole next round."

"There isn't going to be a next round," Brian said, exasperated. "The Thusser are cheating. They're breaking the Rules. They're invading without an official victory. We have to stop them."

"Yeah — yeah — but you're always running off to stop someone from doing something without any plan or any way of protecting yourself. You always just assume I'm going to come save you."

"What do you mean by that?"

"Last night, you would have been grabbed or killed or something by that monster if I hadn't run after you with a rake."

"So I was, like, I was supposed to sit there and watch one of those kids get taken away by the Thusser?" Brian asked hotly, remembering Gregory hanging back in the house, saying there was nothing they could do.

86

"You have to be realistic," said Gregory.

"I am being realistic," said Brian. "I'm just not being selfish."

"That's right," said Gregory. "You're the hero."

They didn't speak for a while. They were both too angry. They walked through the haunted suburbs.

Brian knew he should apologize. He should apologize and then Gregory would apologize and then everything would be right, just like normal. Brian thinking things out, Gregory making jokes. But Brian didn't want to give in. So they didn't speak as they walked along past blank windows and green lawns. They walked past houses where the garage doors had been left open. They walked past houses with toys in the yard.

Eyes watched them. In a house where the couch had been dragged to block the front door and a dining room chair had been shoved under the knob of the back door, a terrified bank teller huddled behind the media hutch, surrounded by bottles of water and pots full of basmati rice. He was hiding. He fearfully kept tabs on the street, eyes blinking. He had not moved from his crouch in several days. He did not know where his wife was. He did not want anyone to come downstairs. He was afraid of what he might see: his wife or something else entirely that had already found her and devoured her. He was afraid of what might be looking for him. He was not sure he was thinking rationally. So he stayed put. When he needed to poo, he used a Pringles tin.

He watched a stocky boy with glasses and a blond kid walk past in the bright sunlight, and he knew that there was something wrong with them. He could feel that they were marked.

He ducked. He dimly recalled that his daughter might be hidden behind the love seat. He slid some rice toward her hiding place. Nothing moved. He hoped she still was there, and that she hadn't disappeared while he was asleep.

Outside, beneath blue skies, Brian and Gregory did not notice anyone watching. They walked through the dazed subdivision. They turned a corner. A hose fed a wading pool that had already overflowed. Farther down the street, a chimney lay on a perfect lawn. A grandfather sat in a garage, door open, moaning. He sat on bags of fertilizer.

They began to peer about more carefully. Something was wrong.

The feeling was different than the day before. It was not peaceful. It felt unquiet, disrupted.

They passed a house that had no doors to get in or out. Without speaking, they both surveyed its surfaces, going around a corner, noting blank wall after blank wall. The windows had shades drawn.

One lawn was wildly overgrown. Ragweed poked through the struts of a plastic fun slide.

They passed the soccer field. There was a game going on, which meant it might be Saturday. But the kids were crawling up the field, dragging themselves as if the field were vertical, and the ball sat alone, unkicked. The adults on the sidelines sobbed.

Brian and Gregory watched. Gregory played soccer, so he would have recognized if any of the crawling had been regulation. The kids dug their fingers into the earth and pulled themselves along. They panted.

"Let's go," said Brian, darkly.

"What's going on?" whispered Gregory.

"I don't know," said Brian.

He stared at the weeping parents.

The Game had been frightening enough. But this — whatever was happening now was beyond the Rules. And if, all of a sudden, all the Rules were off, then anything could happen. Nothing protected Prudence, wherever she was. Nothing protected Brian and Gregory. And evil could very easily win.

Brian kept his thoughts to himself. He figured Gregory wouldn't want to hear them. Gregory, for his part, knew that there was something that Brian wasn't saying. So the two boys walked on through the landscape in silence.

They passed identical streets. New mailboxes were knocked down. Drapes were pulled tight to block out the day. There was an air of emptiness, even when people passed them in cars.

At last, they came to the construction. Earthmovers were rumbling and jolting over the mounds. It seemed like, since the previous day, there were already new units, laid out on the grass like a picnic.

As they were crossing the wasteland of Caterpillar tracks and PVC piping, Brian saw something out of the corner of his eye. Glittering parked cars, he thought.

He pointed without speaking. Neither of the two really wanted to break his silence. They walked across the churned-up lots.

As they walked, Brian looked at stumps and ground roots under his feet. He wondered where they were on the map of the old Game. He couldn't recognize the landmarks anymore. Everything was erased. He couldn't recall exactly how the paths had led.

He became more anxious as they approached what looked at first like a parking lot.

It was not a parking lot.

Gregory swore when he saw, and they both started running.

TWELVE

Cars — many of them — were scattered all over the razed field. There was no order to them — no rows, no tidy schemes. Several of the cars were running, blue fumes drifting up around them. The sun shone down on them.

It was not the cars that startled Gregory and Brian, but the people. Many of them were lying in the mud around the cars, as if they'd suffered seizures or been mowed down by guns.

"See — this," said Gregory, running beside Brian, "is an instance where I believe in running *away*."

Brian reached a silver Volvo sports wagon next to which a man lay prone. Brian stooped beside him.

The man was breathing. His eyes were partially open. He did not seem wounded.

"Hello?" said Brian. "Sir? Sir?"

The man didn't respond. Gregory squatted down on the other side of him. "What's wrong with him?" the boy asked.

Brian didn't respond, but reached out gingerly and shook the man's shoulder. It was caked with mud. "Sir?" he said again.

The man stirred like a child in sleep, reluctant to leave a dream of wonders. "I'm at work right now," he said, slurring. "Can I call you later?"

"You're in a field of mud," Gregory insisted. "You're lying beside a car."

The man turned onto his side, facing away from Gregory. He rubbed his face with his hand and stopped moving. He clearly didn't want to be disturbed.

"You should get up," said Brian. "You're lying with part of you in a puddle."

The man pulled his knees up against his chest, dragging his calves and cuffs through the oily water. He closed his eyes and whispered a demand that something be collated pronto.

Brian and Gregory stood. They wandered around the graveyard of commuters. People were slumped at the wheels of their cars. Men lay in the dirt, their shirts half untucked from writhing in sleep, their ties twisted beneath them, grimy with mud. Women rested against the wheels of their coupes, mouths open, breathing loudly. The two boys walked quietly between them, their shoes squelching in ruts.

A summer breeze blew over the desolation. The hair of insensate middle managers stirred and fluttered.

"What is this?" Gregory whispered. Then he yelled, "HELLO?"

His voice seemed small in a very large plain.

"They think they're at the office," said Brian. "All of them, I bet. At the office or the grocery store or something."

"What . . . why?"

"They're hypnotized somehow. Because they can't leave the neighborhood. If they left, they'd realize what was going on. They'd be able to tell that time was passing differently."

"So they just come here?" said Gregory. "They leave for work, they just drive over here, and then they fall asleep until it's time to go home?"

"Otherwise, the Thusser wouldn't be able to keep them in the development. People would leave and they'd realize that time was weird and that they were confused. They wouldn't come back."

Gregory shook his head. He was aghast. He didn't like to think that things could go this wrong.

One family in the lot was clearly on vacation. There were kayaks on the roof, bikes on the racks, and parents in the front seats, asleep on the dashboard. In the backseat, kids were canted against the windows, their cheeks smeared on the glass. They were ready for swimming.

Brian and Gregory pounded on the windows. They pummeled the doors. There was no motion within the car. Frantically, the two of them charged around the muddy lot and shook people lying on the ground. No movement. The heads rolled unevenly. The arms slumped. The bodies were heavy as sacks of sand.

Gregory rarely had the chance to slap a few faces, especially in public, but now he could slap away, leaning down and yelling long and loud, one screaming note right in the ear of a man in dress jeans, hollering at him with a look of desperation, a desperation that seemed born of an astonished irritation that anyone could get mesmerized this way, that anyone could be so dumb. He just couldn't believe that they wouldn't wake up.

Brian watched him, sadly.

When Gregory had exhausted himself, he stood up. His knees were capped with mud. He and Brian stood in the field, surrounded by duped dreamers. In the distance, the sound of cicadas started up in the trees.

Solemnly, Brian and Gregory walked away from the parking lot. Then, without discussing it, they both began to run. An eagle was in the air over their heads, looking for the woodland. They reached the construction. Workmen with uneven mouths watched them pass.

Brian and Gregory headed for the sales office, where Milton Deatley, deceased, was open for business.

THIRTEEN

In the waiting room of the business office, on a cheap wood pedestal, stood the noble elk himself, a look of deep compassion in his glass eyes, the summer sunlight catching and spinning on his polypropylene antlers.

The office itself was converted from one of Rumbling Elk Haven's six unique house designs. The waiting room would normally have been a living room, and there was not much to distinguish it from a living room (it had couches, chairs, a coffee table with real estate magazines carefully overlapping in diagonals), except for the plastic elk and, near the fireplace, a laminated map on an easel.

Brian went over to the map immediately and began to study it. Gregory stood awkwardly by the elk. Smooth jazz was playing in the air.

No one was at the reception desk.

"The Crooked Steeple!" Brian exclaimed. "I forgot about it. It's just up the hill from Prudence's house."

"What about it?" asked Gregory.

"It's still there. It's on the map. I mean, it's surrounded by houses, but it's a landmark that could help us figure out what's —"

"I was getting some coffee," said a woman, coming through a door. "And throwing away the rest of my breakfast burrito." She walked to the desk and sat on it, crossing her legs. Her hair was sprayed into a mane. "Are your parents around?"

Brian said no; Gregory, thinking more quickly, said, "They're outside. They'll be here in a minute."

The receptionist looked carefully from one boy to the other. "So your parents are outside."

"They're walking around."

"That's great. We encourage walking."

"It strengthens the hams."

"The hams," the woman repeated. "Do you kids want some comic books to look at while you wait?"

Brian blurted, "Is Mr. Deatley here?"

The woman walked behind her desk and sat down in her chair. "Why do you want to see Mr. Deatley?"

"He's a friend of my parents," said Gregory. "He took a parachuting class with my dad."

The woman looked skeptical. "I didn't know Milt parachuted."

"Oh, you can drop him from all kinds of heights," Gregory attested.

The woman asked, "Do you want anything from the kitchen while you wait? We have Danish."

"I'll take a Danish," said Gregory.

"We're not really hungry," Brian answered.

"We'd like to see Mr. Deatley," Gregory insisted.

"He's not here right now," the woman said, "in the actual office."

Gregory asked, "Is he okay?"

"Sure, he's fine."

"Looking good? My dad was worried about him. He said the last time he saw him, he looked kind of like a corpse."

"He's great."

"You know, the walking dead."

Brian muttered, "Gregory."

"He's out and about," the woman said. "He's checking out some units over on Heather Lane."

Gregory asked, "Is there a problem?"

"With what?"

"On Heather Lane?"

The receptionist smiled irritably. "There's no problem. We do our best to resolve any issues swiftly and to the satisfaction of all our owners."

"We'll head over there," said Brian.

The receptionist seemed suspicious. "Won't your parents miss you?"

Gregory said, "They'll find us."

"You better leave a note."

"No, that's fine."

The boys slipped out before she could ask any more questions.

"Did you have to make jokes?" Brian asked.

"She didn't notice."

"Yes she did. She could tell you were lying."

"No she couldn't. She was thinking about those Danish."

Brian shook his head angrily. He said, "Let's go. It's over this way. I memorized the map." He began running along the road.

"Oh, did you?" said Gregory. "And what are we going to do when we meet Milton Deatley? Don't we want to have a story?"

"We have to find out about Prudence."

"We can't just ask him. We should have broken into his office and looked around. While she was throwing away her breakfast burrito."

Brian realized Gregory was right. "I don't know what we're going to do when we meet him," he admitted. "We'll have to play it by ear."

"You haven't seen many zombie movies, have you?" said Gregory. "Otherwise, you wouldn't talk about meeting the undead and playing it by ear. Or any phrase involving body parts." They turned left down a half-paved gravel road. "Like pulling his leg," Gregory continued. They turned right onto tarmac. "Or whether him meeting with us is any 'skin off his back.'"

"Thanks," said Brian. He didn't want to joke around.

"You're just grumpy because you're the *brains* of the outfit. You're basically a menu item for zombies."

Past driveways and Palladian windows they jogged, past empty lawns and chilly concrete birdbaths. They saw no one on the streets.

Brian slowed his run. He was breathing heavily. They were in the heart of the suburb.

They stepped onto Heather Lane.

The road was curiously silent.

The houses looked uninhabited, somehow, though new. Brian couldn't put his finger on why. He and Gregory walked cautiously down the sidewalk. A few cars were abandoned on the street. They had not been parked but were at angles. The door of one was open. The light was no longer on. The car battery had run down.

Something had happened here.

Brian's palms were sweating. He looked to Gregory, who was also silenced by the menace in the air.

They were about halfway along the street when Brian pointed at a house.

At first, Gregory saw only the basketball hoop in the driveway, the miniature soccer net rimmed with Styrofoam. Then he looked past the hydrangeas. He saw something move in the backyard.

Four white horses cropped the grass. They were yoked to a black car with chrome trim.

FOURTEEN

Brian and Gregory approached the house. The front door was open. Brian looked in first and hurled himself back out.

"What?" asked Gregory.

"There's someone in there."

From inside came a soft, hesitant clank.

Gregory approached the open door and looked in. Brian couldn't see past him. Gregory was clearly staring at something in front of him. Gregory said, "Hello. Are you okay?"

A man's voice, thin and whining, replied, "I'm waiting."

"Are you okay?" Gregory insisted. "Is there anything wrong?"

"The kids are already part of it," said the man's voice.

Brian crept up to Gregory's side and peered through the doorway. The dim, moving mound he'd seen when he looked in the first time now resolved itself.

It was a man in a suit. He had prized up the thin marble tiles that lined his entryway and had crawled under them like they were a quilt. He was hunkered on the naked substrate. He peered out from between the stacked, chipped squares, with red, terrified eyes.

"Where's the owner of the horses?" asked Brian.

"Mr. Deatley," the man answered. He clutched at his marble skirts. "A monster came through," he said. "The kids were safe in a wall. Thanks be. Thanks be." He started to cry. "It was a monster." Several of his tiles slid off and went spinning across the splintered floor. Startled, he leaped; more tile jangled and fell. It busted on the backer board. The man shifted, looking about him. "Can you hide me? Can you put more marble on me? High up? The kids are already gone."

"What do you mean, *gone*?" Brian asked. He backed against the door frame. "Where — where do they take them?"

"They're right here," said the man. He was hunched down, stubbing his fingers and thumbs on tiles still embedded in the mortar, trying to pry them loose.

Brian squatted down. "Are they under the house?" he asked gently.

"In the wall," the man whispered back. "They're safe."

A chill went down Brian's spine. "Where?" he asked. "Where are they in the wall?"

"In their room," said the man. "They love it here."

"What was the monster like?" Gregory asked.

The man let forth a querulous whine. He kept drawing tiles to him and stacking them on his back, but at this point, he shook too much to balance it. The marble kept cascading down his flanks.

"It had armor," he said. "It had . . . it was crazy."

Brian asked, "Did it put the kids in the wall?"

The man shook his head, dislodging another tile. It bumped and rattled down his back. "They were safe in the wall. It tried to cut them out. It tried to get them and take them away."

Brian stood. "Let's find them," he said to Gregory.

Once again, heading into danger, saving kids we don't know, Gregory thought to himself. *Only, this time I don't even have a rake.*

Carefully, looking around them constantly, arms spread, the two boys crossed the foyer. The man shivered at their approach.

They walked past him, staring around them. On the wall was a photo of sports cars going around a bend. Gregory stopped for a moment before it.

The man in the floor whispered, "I'm an amateur photographer."

"Where are the kids?" Brian asked.

"Up in Bryson's room," the man answered, without explanation.

The two boys began climbing the steps. They kept their eyes roving from side to side so nothing could leap out at them.

On the stairs there were photos of the Sierra Nevada. Two blond kids stood in a field of flowers.

The boys found the children in the second bedroom they went into.

Gregory saw them and yelped. Brian could only stare. Without thinking, he pawed at the door frame, backing away.

It was not an unusual bedroom, except that everything in it was white. The bed and its comforter were white. There were white cubes filled with action figures and guns. There was a white rug. The goose-necked lamp was white, and it cast a white egg of light across the white walls.

The kids had been absorbed somehow into those walls. The sister hung out of the plaster, her upper body slumped, her arms hanging down, her white-blond hair hanging down, her head drooping. There was no seam between the wall and her body. It appeared that her back, her stomach, her shirt simply flattened into it, and she leached out into the plaster, devoured.

The brother had been almost totally consumed. He was less boy than architecture. Still, the wall bulged a bit in the shape of him, as if he were pressed against a membrane. An elbow jabbed out of the flat. A knee. The features of his face rose out of the blank surface. There was a spray of freckles across his nose that fanned out across the plane. They had scattered as he had been absorbed. The white wall was freckled now.

Around the sister were several brutal slices. Someone had hacked at the plaster where her legs should have been, trying to gouge her free.

Brian walked toward the half girl. Gregory started shaking and wouldn't move. He wondered suddenly — wondered if his cousin had been absorbed like this — if she'd been in the walls the whole time, inches from them while they slept.

Brian went to the girl's side and held his fingertips in front of her face.

"She's breathing," he said. "She's alive."

"What is going *on*?" Gregory demanded. "What *is* this?"

There was a crash downstairs. The boys jumped and realized it was the man's tiles all dropping to earth at once. There were voices. The echoes rang out in the desolate house. "They're upstairs," said the man in the floor. "They're looking after the kids."

Brian and Gregory gaped and peered around wildly. Someone was crossing the foyer. Someone was walking up the stairs. Turning at the landing. Striding up another flight.

Someone walked down the hall, jingling slightly.

Someone entered the room. Brian and Gregory were already gone. Still there were the white bed, the white rug, the white lamp casting its egg of white light across the white-frozen siblings, the freckled wall.

Someone opened the closet.

Brian and Gregory cowered.

The man with the red, ground-up face confronted them.

"I believe I can answer your questions," he said.

FIFTEEN

There was no use hiding in the closet. Gregory and Brian sheepishly stepped out.

The man set down his briefcase and held out his hand to shake. As he did, he introduced himself. "Milton Deatley. Real estate developer. Super to meet you."

Brian didn't move. The man grabbed his hand and shook it. "I know," said Deatley. "Brian Thatz. It's a pleasure. I've seen you before. From a distance. We apparently share a commute."

Deatley looked at Brian's friend. "Gregory Stoffle?" Deatley guessed.

"You're dead," said Gregory.

"And you're rude," said the corpse of Milton Deatley. He reached into the breast pocket of his jacket and pulled out a pamphlet that had been reproduced on a cheap color printer. "Here you go." He handed it to Brian and turned away.

It was a piece of paper folded into three. The title was on the cover flap. *What Humans Need to Know About an Invasion of the Thusser Horde.*

"What is this?" Brian whispered.

The corpse of Milton Deatley did not answer. He put his briefcase on the bed and opened it. There were no papers inside, only raw meat.

"Where's my cousin?" Gregory demanded.

"It's all in there," said Deatley, pointing vaguely toward the pamphlet before turning his attention away from the boys.

The corpse reached into his briefcase and pulled out a handful of meat. He walked over to the boy in the bedroom wall, stuck his fingers into the boy's half-glimpsed mouth, and pried it open. He roughly arranged the tongue. He shoved in meat, then manipulated the lower jaw to force it to chew. Beneath the lumpy chin, the wall puckered and smoothed.

"What are you . . . doing?" Gregory protested in horror. Deatley didn't even look at him. He fed the kid another mouthful of meat.

Brian opened the pamphlet and began to read.

What Humans Need to Know About an Invasion of the Thusser Horde

As a human, you might be asking questions about the Thusser settlement of your world. You might be asking, "But what does this mean for *me*?" The answer is almost total annihilation. This pamphlet is designed to put your mind at rest by answering some commonly asked questions about the settlement and what will follow.

What's Going On?

You may feel confused or concerned about changes that have been going on in your neighborhood. That's perfectly natural. The fabric of your world is becoming increasingly thin as we prepare your region for settlement. Time has stopped working as it usually does. The cycle of days is different as we accommodate your world to our own very different chronological landscape. Soon, all will be prepared, and the Thusser will enter this world and take possession of the houses we are constructing here. And these three square miles are only the beginning.

Brian felt a chill of horror at the friendly, informative tone of the pamphlet. He looked up at the corpse of Milton Deatley. Deatley picked up another handful of meat and walked over to the girl who hung out of the wall. With the heel of his other hand, he shoved the girl's forehead up. Her mouth hung open. He crammed it full of meat and forced her to chew.

Brian and Gregory read on in the nightmare brochure.

Can my friends, my family, and I escape before you arrive?

Unfortunately, that's not possible. Because if you've gotten this pamphlet — well, we've arrived! Many of your friends and family members have probably already been absorbed by their houses. We can't let them go. They're part of the preparation. They're part of the neighborhood — a neighborhood, after

107

all, *is* people! We need them. We need their spirits, their dreams. That is part of the atmosphere we breathe. They are what we build our foundations on. They are the dirt into which we pound our tent pegs. We cannot remain in this world without one foot in the dreams of humanity. So each house will have its slumbering humans. After a while, they'll stop dreaming entirely. They'll just be appliances like any other. By that time, the settlement will have spread across North America. There are millions of us waiting to come through. In fact, we've been waiting for centuries!

But that means you're breaking the Rules! You're moving into Norumbegan territory!
Yes, that's true. The Norumbegans are too far away to care. They have their own concerns. They can hardly remember this place. They'll never notice if we move in. Why should we consent to their silly Game when the territory is ripe for the taking? The Thusser Horde needs a place to settle. There's demand. So we're going to move in. It will happen in about three days.

"Where's my cousin?" Gregory demanded.

Brian asked, "Has she been swallowed by her house? Is she in the walls like that?"

"It's all in the brochure," said Deatley. The girl's teeth clacked together as he forced her to chew, then massaged her throat so she'd swallow. "Read."

Brian and Gregory looked down. Indeed, the next question was,

You may be wondering: Where's my cousin?
We like to accommodate our clients here at Rumbling Elk Haven. Your cousin Prudence owned a piece of land right in the middle of our neighborhood, unfortunately. The owners of the units around her thought she might stir up trouble. And we realized she wouldn't harmonize well with our community. So we had her removed.

Has she been absorbed by her house? Is she in the walls?
No. She wasn't willing to be part of what we're trying to do here. She was not a team player. She has been sequestered and is being reworked to ease her transition into the neighborhood.

Gregory went and stood directly in front of the corpse. He shouted, "Where? Where is she?"

The corpse didn't blink. It was, perhaps, incapable of blinking. "I'll take you there, if you like," he said.

"Right now," Gregory insisted.

Deatley stared him down. "You'll never see the light of day again. Think about what you ask for."

Brian said, "You tried to kill me."

Milton Deatley shrugged. "It seemed like a good idea at the time. I thought you might warn the Norumbegans.

109

Luckily, it appears you don't know how." Deatley kept kneading the girl's chin to get her to chew. The meat flecked her lips. "Much more convenient that way. The Norumbegans won't be tipped off until we've already arrived. By then, it will be too late."

"Don't say *we*," said Gregory, defiantly. "You're just a human, too. And not even a live human. A dead human."

Deatley did not respond. He shook his head and wiped his fatty, bloody hand on his pants. He took out a pocket package of Kleenex and plucked one loose. He scrubbed his fingers with it.

Brian saw the pamphlet rearranging itself, the constant fluttering of language on the page.

You are dead. You are human.

This body, yes, is a reconstituted human. I have been rebuilt from the remains of Milton Deatley, deceased. But I am one of the Thusser. I am sitting in a pod, gesturing so this puppet dances on its strings. It was impossible to send in one of the Thusser bodily without setting off alarms. And we needed a human avatar who could make preparations, purchasing the land according to the economic rites of your people. We are an orderly invader. We needed a representative to appear before the zoning board and the town selectmen. For that purpose, we gathered together the pieces of Mr. Deatley and supplied some gobbets to make up the difference. So I only appear to be a real estate developer.

110

I am terrified. I am clutching this brochure, and it creases in my hands as I stand before you. You do not seem to even pay me heed as you go about your business. I do not know what to do when faced by the enormity of your invasion.

Stop worrying! Calm down. Really! There's nothing you can do. We are an infinitely more ancient race than yours, and infinitely wiser. As I speak to you, as I arrange this helpful and informative pamphlet, it is like a kindly human talking to a dog. My signal is infinitely rich. You can't even detect, much less participate in, the excess, all the nuances and extensions to what I'm saying that are at the moment reverberating in this room and rippling through this sheet of paper. A dog can only hear "sit," "lie down," and "walkies." [There was, at this point, full-color clip art of a dog wagging its tail, tongue out.] As you read this, you feel a strange unease — it seems like the ink itself crawls and betrays you — because on some level you are aware that there are many meanings — things unspoken, hieroglyphics in thought. Many are swimming past you, and you are unable to assimilate them. Many more manifest themselves on this page in response to your animal anxieties. I am sorry I cannot make this clearer. You may explain to a dog why you are taking it to the vet for shots, but it will still look at you accusingly when the needle goes in.

So you're saying that if we could only under-stand it, we'd realize this is good for us?
I haven't said anything of the kind. It will essentially obliterate millions of human animals. They will be nothing more than slumbering bundles.

But the Rules —
There are no Rules anymore. Your race likes to func-tion under general agreements. That is necessary because you are all essentially at the same level. But when there is a race far superior to humankind, there is no more need for Rules. There is only dominance.

You can't do this. You have to — you have to go somewhere else. There are other worlds. The Norumbegans found one. You could go to another world and leave us alone.
But why would we? We want to come here.

But we're here.
Why does that matter? You're irrelevant to us. You don't really count. The Thusser Horde wants this place as its own, and we will get it. You're a race far inferior to us. You're useful to us as stepping-stones. Your joy, your sorrows, don't matter to us whatsoever.

You can't even understand the depth of our emotion and how it exceeds yours. The infinitely nuanced mel-ancholies, the bottomless griefs, the joys one of us feels at any given time are more various at once than all of the symphonic pleasures of Rome or Manhattan Isle. Do not think we are a harsh race, unfeeling and terrible. We are a deeply compassionate people — far more than you can ever understand. You are simply not equipped to experience our superiority in this regard. Even as you read and I watch you, standing on the other side of the room with my arms folded, even as I decree your eventual fall and explain its inevitability, I am at the same moment involved in sorrow at your passing as a race and nostalgia for the days of your ascendancy. We plan on including a mural in the community center that recalls humankind and its little joys — going berry picking, hailing buses, excreting, riding the surf on belly boards. All the quaint little behaviors that the Thusser associate with mankind.

The animated corpse of Milton Deatley stood, indeed, with his arms crossed, watching them read, watching the fear grow on their faces.

"But," protested Brian, "you must be able to settle on another world! A different one! It just doesn't make sense!"

"Why? There's this one. We like it. We want it." Milton Deatley threw his dirty Kleenex on the floor, closed his briefcase, and snapped its locks shut. Then he smiled at the two boys. "Anyhoo," he said, "there will be time enough for remorse later. I have mouths to feed. A few more days and they won't need to eat anymore. They will have been completely absorbed. As for you, how about this: You have until nightfall to leave. Go back to Boston.

113

It won't be absorbed for another year or two." He prepared to go. "Remember: Out by nightfall. Or we kill you outright." He grinned. "Okay? I appreciate what you're trying to do, but you really are irrelevant to our effort. Nightfall. That's it. And don't think of warning anyone. It's already too late. Far too late."

He strode out of the room. "Have a great day," he called as he headed down the stairs, leaving Gregory and Brian appalled and alone.

The pamphlet was now blank.

✳ ✳ ✳

For a while, Brian and Gregory couldn't speak. Brian was biting his own lips and staring at the boy in the wall. Gregory sagged on the bed, elbows on his knees, as if all comedy had drained out of him forever. He couldn't look at Brian. To look at Brian would mean he'd have to speak, and Brian would have to speak, and together, they'd have to acknowledge that this was the world they lived in. They would have to start doing something.

Brian got up and went to the girl's side. He examined the slashes in the wallboard. He could not see her legs behind the slashes. It was like she went no farther than the wall itself.

Brian pulled at her arm. She swayed forward. Her head rocked. She didn't respond otherwise. Brian tugged harder. He tried to pull her out of the wall. He said to Gregory, "Come see if we can yank her out."

114

Gregory didn't get up. He looked at Brian once, accusingly, then dropped his gaze to the white rug. They had tracked in mud. It was easy to see how dead Deatley had found them in the closet. Their footprints led right to it.

Brian still pulled at the girl. The wall around her midriff buckled, but more like flesh might.

"Everyone will be like that," said Gregory. "Everyone. Your mom and dad. My mom and dad. Imagine whole streets like this. As far as you can see. People fading into their walls. Or that guy downstairs, trying to fade into his floor. No one talking. No one —"

"I know," said Brian. "I know."

"Well, then stop pulling on that stupid wall girl."

"We need to figure out how to save them."

"You're not going to figure it out from just yanking on her arm."

"I might."

"You won't be —"

But he didn't finish what he was saying.

From downstairs — a tremendous roar — a scream — the man in the floor, squealing, *"MONSTER!"*

Something was sprinting across the foyer.

Something was bounding up the steps, three at a time.

Clad in metal.

Tearing down the hallway.

Screaming with hatred and rage.

Coming right for them.

115

SIXTEEN

It burst into the room. They heard it through the closet door. It was heavy. The floor shook when it stomped.

Gregory slid back farther among the shelved toys, shoving aside a hanging backpack.

"Deatley!" the thing yelled in a voice that was not human.

It threw the door open.

Gregory dropped to the floor and covered his head with his arms.

Brian stood awkwardly on one leg — the other raised slightly in panic — and stared the monster in the eye.

It was about seven feet tall, armed with a huge battle-ax, and encased in a strange armor, curiously wrought, with acanthus inlay on the plates and spikes. The visor of the helmet had a huge, hooked snout, from wherein came the terrifying voice of the giant, which, from a throat inhuman, through fanged teeth, rang in the metal as the beast spoke. It said:

"Brian?"

Brian stared at the giant and its battle-ax. "Kalgrash?" he said.

The monster looked quickly around. "Is, um, Milton Deatley here?"

"He left," said Gregory from the floor.

"Darn." The monster put his ax down. "I wanted to cleave him," he explained. Hands free, he raised his visor.

It was indeed Kalgrash the troll. It was hard not to recognize his spiky nose and uneven, nail-like teeth.

"Kalgrash!" said Brian, jubilantly.

Kalgrash laughed and gave Brian a big hug.

"*Ow!*" said Brian. "*Ow*, your, you know, your plate mail is completely — *ow!*"

"Oh. Sorry," said Kalgrash, releasing the boy. "I'm still not used to being as strong as a hundred oxen."

Gregory stood up. "Great to see you," he said. "You're about three feet taller than last time."

"Milk," said Kalgrash. "Kidding."

"You *are* taller," Brian pointed out. "Way taller."

"Yup, I was, how could you say it, *refitted*?"

"What? How?" Brian asked.

"A while ago — I can't tell how long — I can't tell anything anymore — well . . ." The troll clunked over to the bed and sat down. "We began to see the houses going up, and there was something wrong with them. At first, we thought it was just a normal development. But then Prudence sensed there was something wrong, that there was an eel in the Jell-O, so to speak, and I didn't like how things were going. So I went up to Wee Sniggleping's workshop and I said to him, 'Look here. I think a hard

117

time's coming, and I need to be taller and armored.' So just in time, he fit me up with some new body parts and this armor. I drew it on a piece of paper for him and designed it myself. He just took my crayon drawing and he built all of this to my specifications. It was really nice of him. Then he transferred my . . . you know . . . brain, I guess, and face." Kalgrash paused. "He's gone," he said. "Wee Snig. He's gone. Everything's gone. I haven't been able to find my house for weeks."

"Prudence is gone, too," Gregory said.

"I know. I'm terrified. And these kids," said Kalgrash, gesturing to the kids in the walls. "Look at them. It's awful, awful, awful. They're sleeping like that and there's a great summer day outside. They could be out eating popsicles and playing catch with a very small beagle."

"It's more than popsicles and beagles," Gregory pointed out, still thinking of Prudence.

"I know," said Kalgrash. "Don't tell me. I know, I know, I know. I've been living here, hiding between the houses. And in the cellars. Running around and trying to get people out of their walls and their floors. It doesn't work. They're really *part* of the wall."

"That was you?" said Brian, pointing at the slices near the girl's legs.

"That was stupid me."

"Why were you looking for Milton Deatley?" Gregory asked, a little suspicious.

"To kill him again. I think his corpse is possessed by one of the Thusser. He needs a good smiting. *Wham! Smack! Shklunk!*"

118

Brian would normally have said that a good smiting wouldn't solve anything, but in this case, he suspected a good smiting was a great place to start.

"But that's too much about me. Tell me about you," said Kalgrash. "I haven't seen you in stacks of time. Have you had a good year?"

"Um," said Gregory, "do we really have time for a chat? With sandwiches, and the photo albums laid out on the ottoman?"

"Right," said Kalgrash, standing. The bed creaked as he rose.

"We're here to find Prudence," said Brian. "Then we have to somehow stop the Thusser Horde from set-tling here."

"You have a plan! Hunky-dory!"

"'Hunky-dory'?" said Gregory. "When is that even . . . *from*?"

"I'm a troll dressed in Renaissance battle armor. Don't get snitty about when things are from. Let's get out of here. We may still have time to catch Deatley. I saw his hearse outside."

"Great," said Brian. "He just . . ." He didn't know how to describe what they'd just seen. He didn't want to think about it. So he simply said, "Let's go."

Gregory looked ill. But Kalgrash grinned, slammed down his visor, gripped his ax with both hands, and led the charge.

With that, they set out to catch the undead developer.

SEVENTEEN

They ran out the sliding doors and into the back-yard. The grass looked sparse. Several young trees had been planted in rings of wood chips, supported by cables. The white horses weren't there.

Milton Deatley was already gone.

The two kids and their troll pal ran back and forth, checking to see if Deatley was farther down the street. There was no sign of him, except the pale tracks of his wheels across the crushed grass.

"All right, we spent too much time greeting each other joyfully," said Kalgrash, miffed. "Next time, smite first, hug later."

"Can he be killed . . . again?" said Gregory. "If you run into him?"

Kalgrash shrugged, his shoulders rattling. "At least he can be chopped up into little enough pieces that he can't lurch around the place. So . . . now that I have some backup, I say we go rescue Prudence and Wee Snig."

Brian asked, "You know where they are?"

"No," said Kalgrash. "Not know as in 'know.' But I bet they're underground. In the ruins of the city under the mountain. A few weeks before Prudence disappeared, she visited me. I was still short. I was in my cave back then. I loved that cave. It was the best cave on cold winter nights. I loved sitting down there near the fire."

"Okay," said Gregory impatiently.

"So Prudence comes by, and she tells me she's worried, because she thinks that the development around her house is moving awful fast, and she's not sure it's normal. And she's just been down in the City of Gargoyles, and she says that there are big things growing on the sides of some of the houses."

"Things?" Brian asked.

"Like sacs. Sacs were growing on the sides of houses down in the city. Do you remember the city? With all the crazy carvings?"

"Sure," said Brian. "What kind of sacs?"

"Like gray mushrooms. Growing all over the place. And she was worried that they were growths from some other world, you know, like spores that had blown into our world through one of the holes left around here, and then they start to get big down there. So anyway, she talked about that. And then about a week later — at least, I think it was a week, but time is all confused nowadays. You never know when the sun is going to set or come up. *Grrr, grrr, grrr.* Anyway, by my reckoning, a week later, she comes back and says she's been down there again, and the fungi are larger. Much larger. And she told me that something was seriously wrong, something

121

was invading. I was already getting worried, so I had talked to Sniggleping about getting body extensions so I could do smiting. It's a good thing, too, because that night the earthmovers started to rip away the top of my burrow — you know, my kitchen? — and I ran out screaming and yelling, but the workmen didn't stop or even notice me, and I kept swinging my ax around and breaking stuff and *hcha! cha! pfwam!* That slowed them down a little, but then this creature was there that hardened every time I hit it, so I couldn't stop it, and it kept on attacking, and it tore me up pretty bad, and I just managed to escape and —"

"We killed it," said Gregory, proudly. "We figured out how to kill it. It was pretty easy, really."

"You killed *one*," Kalgrash corrected. "They've got a bunch of them. They call them *kreslings*."

Brian asked, "Who are the people actually building the houses? Are they human?"

"All mesmerized or hypnotized or something," said Kalgrash. "Undead Deatley controls them all. Can I go on with my story, in which our charming troll hero has been battered and torn up by a monster and is running for safety, close to death? Or is it not exciting enough for you?"

"We know you lived," said Gregory sourly.

"You don't know that. I could be dead."

"You're not dead."

"Deatley's dead, and he's more spry than I am."

"Um, Kalgrash?" said Brian. "Could we just hear the rest of your story?"

"Oh. So, my leg is broken, and my chest has been slashed up, and I'm in all this pain."

"You're not in pain," said Gregory.

"I'm in pain. I was there. In pain."

Gregory said harshly, "You can't feel pain."

Kalgrash looked at Gregory with an anger approaching hatred. He said, very distinctly, "It feels to me like I can feel pain. You can call it a mechanical failure, if you like."

Gregory was a little taken aback by Kalgrash's anger. He didn't interrupt again.

"So. The stupid machine troll goes up the mountain, pulling himself along, because he stupidly believes he's in pain. And though he's starting to lose consciousness, he gets to Wee Sniggleping's workshop before he collapses. He passes out. Having just lived through a ferocious attack. And having seen his own home destroyed. Which *seems*, to *him*, like it makes him really intensely sad and angry. Even though he's a *machine*."

"Gregory didn't mean that," said Brian.

"What did he mean?"

"I didn't mean to be a jerk," said Gregory, uncomfortably. "I don't know why I said it."

"Can I continue?" said Kalgrash.

Brian said, "Kalgrash, you're not a machine. You're our friend." He glared carefully at Gregory.

"When I woke up, it was a couple of days later. Snig had built me taller. According to my specifications. With armor accessories. So I bounded back down the mountain, but I couldn't find my house anymore, or where it

123

used to be. There were just houses — houses, houses, houses. All over the place. So I had to hide so the humans wouldn't see me. I hid in little ditches and near the river and things, looking for my burrow. I decided to go back up the mountain and ask Sniggleping what was going on. I get to his lair, and the door's open. Nothing's there. It's been cleaned out or he's evacuated. I didn't know what to do. I didn't know if something had happened and I hadn't been told. So I ran down the mountain and went to Prudence's house. I knocked on her back door and she let me in, and she said she had a really bad feeling that Sniggleping had been taken away. She thought that something was living down in the caverns and had taken him prisoner down there. She tried scrying for him, and she got an image. It looked like he was in the dungeons under the old Norumbegan palace. I told her I'd go down and look around. I went out to try to spelunk but I couldn't figure out where the entrances into the caverns were anymore. I mean, I used to know them all, but the whole landscape is different now that there are all these houses. I walked around and around but it was just backyards and lawns and garages.

"So I went back to Prudence's house to tell her she'd have to help me find a way into the mountain. I got there at about midnight. Her car was there, but she didn't answer. I went in and searched the place. Nobody. I waited for her for a day. The sun rose and came through the windows onto the carpet and I sat there waiting, and then the sun went down on the other side of the house and she still wasn't there. It was creepy. Something was wrong. Really wrong. When I went back out, I saw people were getting stuck in their houses or taken away at night. So I started to try to save them. But people — humans — they tend not to believe trolls when we say, 'Come here! Run, quick! Run for safety!'"

Brian nodded somberly.

"And recently I've been looking for a way down into the caverns, because I bet that somewhere down there, Prudence and Sniggleping are being held. I've been walking around at night, when I won't be seen, but I can't find any of the old landmarks. Now it doesn't even matter, daytime or nighttime. Nobody notices. Everything is so crazy that a troll walking down the street doesn't seem unusual."

"So we need to get down into the caverns, you think," said Brian. "Down to the prison cells under the palace."

"That's where I think they are. That's where Prudence guessed Snig had been taken, and my gut tells me she's right." He looked pointedly at Gregory. "You know, I pretend to have a gut."

"I said I'm sorry."

"Actually, you didn't."

"Well, I meant to say it."

Kalgrash looked down. "Does a potbelly count as a gut?"

Brian said, "Kalgrash, you're one of the most alive people I know."

"We can stop talking about me and start talking about getting subterranean. Now, where do you remember the entrances to the caverns being?"

"That sort of gazebo thing," said Gregory.

"Fundridge's Folly," Brian recalled. "And then there was an entrance hidden in the Ceremonial Mound. In all of those pine trees. And there was a stairway from the top of the mountain down into Snarth's Cavern."

"Okay," said the troll. He thought for a moment. "That's what I remember. So. Which one's closest?"

"Well, where are we now?" said Brian. "Roughly?"

They looked around them. Nothing but houses, lawn, sunlight. Brian walked the route in his mind from the River of Time and Shadow . . . through the Tangled Knolls . . . all those little mounds and hillocks . . . and then that street that ran through the Tangled Knolls. . . . It hadn't been a street, though, he didn't think. . . . It wasn't paved, it was . . . He thought harder. It was a path. A forest path. He remembered that much. Or had it been paved? Had it been just dirt, or was it a sidewalk? He knew he remembered houses there. . . . So a sidewalk made sense. . . . But there couldn't have been houses. It was the forest . . . it was . . .

"I can't remember anything," said Kalgrash. "I'm trying to remember the way we used to go through the neighborhood to get to the mountain, and I can't. I am sure it used to be forest, but I can only catch a glimpse."

Brian knew what the troll meant. He recalled the shape of trees against the morning sky . . . branches . . . a clearing . . . the path an invitation . . . yes, those branches, growing like that, with one splayed out and some bushes on either side . . . and he tried to hold on to them, but then recalled a clapboard wall behind them. And if he focused

126

for a second on that clapboard wall, tried to recall how exactly it looked, he found his memory of trees evaporated.

"This is what it's been like," complained the troll, knocking his own barbaric skull with his fist. "The Thusser are settling in our minds. They're moving into our memories."

Brian tried harder and harder to recall the look of the Haunted Hunting Grounds, where once the gentry of Norumbega and their Emperors had ridden in cavalcade, wimpled and crowned, horses caparisoned and bedecked with cloth of gold — and he saw them hemmed in by pastel porches, or pausing nobly in living rooms, a shaft of light falling through the panes of a Palladian window to glint upon a fair steed's barding as some knight wandered past the units of a sectional sofa.

He could not recall how the forest had looked before the coming of the houses.

"I can't remember anything," he admitted. "I can't . . ."

Gregory asked, "Are you sure that there weren't houses there? I think there were a few in those Haunted Hunting Grounds."

"That's what I remember," said Kalgrash. "But I can't remember the name of the road."

Brian didn't think they were right. He really didn't. He recalled — or did he? — a sea of lilies of the valley. Or one. At least one lily of the valley. Near a concrete foundation. Had that house been built yet? Or just the foundation? He couldn't fix it in his mind.

"The one on top of the mountain, I remember," said

Brian. "That one was way up there. I know there weren't any houses."

"Are you sure?" said Gregory. "Didn't we sleep on someone's porch up there? When we escaped from Snarth? That ogre with the strong sense of smell?"

"No," said Brian. "We slept on . . . I think it was a construction site. They must have just started to build things then. I bet we can find it, though. If we just go straight up the side of the mountain. I bet we can still find that one. It's clearer than the others."

"Okay," said Gregory.

Kalgrash nodded. "Let's go," he said.

They began walking toward the mountain, and whatever awaited them there.

EIGHTEEN

They did not make it far. As they passed along the streets toward the mountain, the houses became more derelict. The doors were open. Cars were haphazard. A sofa had been dragged out and savaged. Fluff from its innards blew down the driveway, tickling the tar, and scummed up a drain.

Gregory looked impossibly grim. His mouth was flat and his eyes tracked suspiciously from one side to the other.

Kalgrash, too, seemed distracted. "Do you think I need a plume on this helmet?" he murmured to Brian. "I think that would look great. The cherry on the cupcake, you know?"

Looking around the haunted neighborhood, Brian asked, "Where are the people?"

"Go in and look," said Kalgrash.

"We don't need to," said Gregory. "You tell us."

"They start by making forts. They're scared. They make forts and hide themselves in their furniture. You

129

know, stacks of pillows. Or they topple over the sofa and then haul a love seat on top of it. And they hide there, just crouching there, without any food or water, just them hiding and getting hungrier and weirder. As I said, if you're a troll, it doesn't really make sense to try to coax them out. Frightened people find that kind of talk unconvincing, coming from trolls. And so they stick closer and closer to one spot. And then finally, after some days, they just lie down wherever they are and stop saying anything. They start to get absorbed, like those kids back there."

Gregory put his hand over his mouth and did not take it away.

"You haven't answered a person's questions about plumes," said Kalgrash, but no one was in the mood to discuss his helm.

The enormity of their task weighed on them. This was no Game played for a forgotten race. It was humanity's problem now, and Gregory and Brian were the only ones who knew about it, and there was no adult to intervene or protect.

Brian could understand why people hid in their houses, why they lurked beneath their love seats, gripped what they knew, and tried to forget.

And Gregory, beside him, peered from side to side, and wished to reach the basements of the mountain as quickly as possible, and find Prudence and Snig, and hand the whole awful mess off to them so it would no longer be his responsibility. He walked ahead of the others, wary, surveying windows.

The houses they passed began to get stranger, distorted. Brian and Gregory stopped and stared. "It gets weirder," Kalgrash explained, "the closer you get to the center. They've had longer to be absorbed."

The houses billowed. They did not seem to be solid. Their proportions were odd, stretched thin, warped, and their windows shuddered like bubbles.

Another street along, whole walls fluctuated and breathed. In their midst were lumps — humans caught up in the flesh of the place, dreaming away while the houses slowly ballooned and exhaled.

The boys and the troll pressed on.

It was clear to Brian, to Gregory, that everything was being prepared for occupation by the Thusser. These were Thusser houses now, spreading out long bat wings to meet one another, growing nests in their depths where the Thusser might curl in time spent immobile. The yards themselves trembled.

Brian was astounded. Gregory was too horrified to make cheap jokes. Kalgrash had seen it before, but remained reverently silent now in the face of the disaster.

A few more streets along, they saw the center of the maelstrom — the door into the Thusser world, ready to open. The lawns were yanked like emerald sheets, rucked up into a vortex. The sails of nearby houses rippled in otherworldly winds. Slowly, everything tended toward that tight, churning point at the center of the whirlpool of earth — a green, suffocated spot.

"Let's go into the center of it," said Gregory.

131

"That would be a really bad idea," Kalgrash warned.

Gregory's voice was dead, somehow pallid. He said, "It would be great to go in there. Just to see."

"No," said Kalgrash. "It would be kind of awful and you wouldn't live. You'd be pulled apart or something and you'd come out the other end all scissored up."

Gregory didn't heed the troll. He began walking toward the center of the whirlpool. He moved like a dreamer. As he walked, the ground got spongier. His sneakers sank.

"No!" said Brian. "Don't, Gregory! Come on!"

Gregory didn't pay any attention to his friend. He walked onward, unresponsive.

"Oh well," said Kalgrash, leaning on his battle-ax. "We tried our hardest."

Brian didn't think they'd tried at all. He ran toward his friend, yelling at him to stop. The dirt beneath his feet was soft and yielding. The air was thin, and a strong gust blew him back.

Gregory was walking in a spiral, following the long, galactic arms of the maelstrom.

Brian saw that as Gregory got closer to the center, to the hole into the Thusser world, he walked faster and faster — impossibly fast.

Brian ran straight toward him, ignoring the ridges beneath his feet.

He didn't seem to be getting any closer. Gregory was whirring along — sleepwalking — racing.

Brian realized: Gregory was sped up. As he approached the Thusser world, time was changing. The closer Gregory got to the portal, the faster he'd go.

Brian ran as fast as he could — straight toward Gregory — ignoring the spiral — his feet pounding on the squish of alien loam.

Still, he wasn't gaining on Gregory . . . no faster . . . Brian hurled himself forward. . . .

And he realized, suddenly, that though it seemed to him like he was making a straight line for Gregory, he, too, was following the spiral. Straight had somehow become profoundly curved.

He didn't know what to do. Gregory, taking little, dazed steps, was flying along like a dizzy hero in a silent film. Brian himself was running as fast as possible and — there came Kalgrash's voice — drooling slow from a block away — unintelligibly slow.

So Brian hurled himself sideways. He began to jolt to one side, instead of running straight toward Gregory. He hurled himself again and again to the right, though it seemed like he was at an angle from his friend.

He stumbled. Flew — felt static — jumped up — collapsed — rose — hurled himself.

He was doing it. He was making it sideways through the spirals.

Kalgrash was frozen, leaping, far behind him.

Gregory was almost at the eye. The lawns folded and creased into the hungry gate, the mouth of the other world.

Brian hurled himself sideways once again. He was only inches from Gregory. He reached out to grab him, time stretching impossibly — going faster for his fingers, for his wrist, for his elbow, itching, up the arm. His hand

133

whapped backward as if blown by water, events moving too quickly for Brian to control the muscles.

Brian tried again to reach for Gregory.

He couldn't jam his hand against the flow of time.

He tried again.

And Gregory, in his trance, got closer to the gateway that would tear him apart.

NINETEEN

As they approached the center of the maelstrom, the gate to another world, wind roared down the arms of the spiral. At this point, the grassy ground was so soft that Gregory sank ankle deep at every step, swaying. A few more feet and he'd be at the point where the ground collapsed into the tunnel that led to the Thusser world.

Brian tried again to grab Gregory's shoulder. His hand tingled with the interference of time and was knocked back once more. Brian could tell that what seemed straight *toward* Gregory was not straight at all.

Brian tried to throw himself sideways again. This time, the jolt as he passed from time-slip to time-slip was ferocious, and he felt sick as his own blood jammed and thinned in circulation.

But he was parallel with Gregory now. Gregory was exactly one cycle faster and closer than Brian.

Brian stuck out his arm. It refracted, appearing in a different spot in the air than he expected.

He withdrew it.

Gregory seemed like he was in a trance. He walked without even noticing Brian's attempts to save him.

Brian saw what he had to do. Instead of trying to pull Gregory back, he had to block Gregory and push him.

Brian calculated the direction in which time was bending his limbs. He thrust his arm sideways again, adjusting for the distortion.

It appeared in front of Gregory, bent impossibly by time and shifting space. Brian's calculations were correct. Gregory stumbled against the hand. His stumble, given his supernatural speed, was comedic. He fell, knees up. Looked around. Saw the hole into another world only a couple of feet away. It burned green, as if nauseated by its swallowing.

Brian had withdrawn his arm. It was too dangerous to leave it going faster than his body. It was turning purple, falling asleep. He yelled, as quickly he could, "Gregory comebackit'sdangerouscomebackherecomebacknow!"

Gregory seemed to have woken up. He glanced in terror at the hole into the other world. He began crab-crawling backward, like a nature film sped up.

Brian watched Gregory try to move straight away from the hole in the earth. In fact, he moved on a curve, space being bent into a spiral.

The two of them trod the path backward. They passed houses swaying in the interdimensional breeze. The ground got harder. Trees bobbed. Alien things were wound in their branches — things that had already slithered over from beyond. Dark little eyes watched the boys fight the breeze. Tiny little claws stitched their way along the bark.

Another ten minutes, and the distortions in time and space had slowed. The boys no longer had to struggle to figure out which way they were walking.

They were just crossing a lawn near a weird, shuddering house.

"That was really kind of funny," said Kalgrash. "I mean, the way you looked all fast like that."

"What happened?" said Brian. "You could've been lost forever."

"Thanks. I know that," said Gregory.

"I was just asking what —"

"Something . . . I don't know what." Gregory hesitated, trying to think back to why he'd made a run for the portal. "It wasn't my idea," he finished peevishly.

"We're all confused," said Brian.

"Some of us are more confused than others," said Kalgrash, raising his eyebrows.

Gregory shot him an irritable look. "At least I know where my house is."

"At least if I see time's giant, gaping nostril, I don't run and dive into it."

"Let's keep going," said Brian. The last thing he wanted was to take sides on this one. "We have to get away from the suburb by the time darkness falls, remember."

Kalgrash grumbled, "I hope there's some smiting soon."

"Don't worry," said Gregory. "There will be."

✳ ✳ ✳

Fifteen minutes later, houses were settling down again. The alien elements — the weird membranous architecture of the Thusser — were diminishing, and walls were staying put. Carefully, Brian, Gregory, and Kalgrash moved away from the center of the development.

They were having a hard time, however, heading straight for the mountain. First, it was not always visible. Second, the streets never seemed to go exactly the way they wanted them to. Third, the sun was starting to set.

"It seems like it should still be morning," said Gregory.

Brian said, "I don't get it exactly. If time is slowed down in here, the days should seem longer, but instead they go really quick."

And indeed, though the kids were just getting hungry for lunch, and it was summer, when the days should be long, evening was falling. The boys and the troll walked along streets bronzed with low-slanted light. Trees cast shadows of trunks askance across clapboards. Cars were rolling back into the neighborhood, nosing toward their homes. People strolled down their driveways, their business suits blistered with mud from their day's hypnotic snooze.

No one seemed to notice a troll begirt like a conquistador, strolling down their street. A cat even came up to him and scampered along gleefully by his ankles.

"The place doesn't look so menacing, now," said

138

Kalgrash. He waved at a drugged-looking financial planner who was pulling elfin circulars out of his mailbox.

"Except," Gregory pointed out, "sundown is when we have to be out or the Thusser try to kill us in earnest."

"We've got to get to the mountain by then," Brian said. "Let's walk faster."

They did, Kalgrash's armor clanking.

"So," Kalgrash said, "the Thusser are cheating. Breaking the Rules."

"That's what we think," said Brian.

"The Norumbegans will be angry. If only we could find some way to tell them."

"There must be a way," said Brian. "Isn't there? Prudence never told me . . . I should have studied all of this harder. Here we are, and I don't know hardly anything about spells or magic."

"How is it coming along, the Game?" the troll asked. "I mean, it's yours, isn't it?"

"Yeah," said Gregory. "It's his." Gregory didn't sound very happy about that.

Kalgrash said, "Well, he won. That's all I mean."

Gregory explained, "I let him win."

Brian felt a little flare of anger. But he didn't want to be a jerk to Gregory when Gregory was already depressed for having lost, so he didn't say anything.

He just said, "My round was going to be a mystery. I love mystery books, so it was going to be a whole thing with detectives and mobsters. And then the players would find out that the mobsters were mythological, and they'd have to put together clues. I worked out all these clues. I guess it won't happen now, though."

"Don't say that."

"The Thusser are breaking the Rules," Brian insisted. "It's not going to matter anymore, what I made up."

"You were really excited about running the Game."

Gregory said, "Of course, he was."

"It doesn't matter," said Brian. "Awful things are happening to people here. Much worse than the Game. I can't believe the Norumbegans would risk everything like they did. . . ."

"You can still be proud of what you were going to do," said Kalgrash. "You won, kiddo!"

"We both won," said Gregory. "I mean, not technically, but we agreed that Brian had to win."

"He won," Kalgrash insisted.

"I just," Brian confided, "I just . . . I pictured what it would be like to set up a session of the Game, and then I hoped that the Norumbegan player would win, and that the Norumbegans would return. I imagined them coming back from the other world — all of them shining, like we've seen them. They're all dressed cool, and they just look . . . well, you know, you've seen them. And I pictured them coming back, and thanking us for saving their kingdom for them. And then maybe we'd meet the other people who've arranged the Game over the years. And maybe we could see the City of Gargoyles when it was full of people instead of ghosts. We could visit it whenever we wanted, and there'd be this whole secret world. . . . And now, you know — none of that."

140

Kalgrash didn't say anything. He nodded sympathetically, and his armor quietly clanked.

"But like I said. It doesn't matter. All these people are trapped here now. They don't even know what's happening to them."

Gregory said, "They don't even know there's a flipping troll walking by right in front of them."

"Do you see?" said Kalgrash. "I'm waving like the Queen of England. Cup hand . . . turn at the wrist . . . turn at the wrist . . . turn at the wrist. . . ."

They walked down the middle of the road. The streets were golden now. The first lights were coming on in houses where families sat down to dinner, or watched television, or performed the quiet deeds of evening. The ovals of glass in front doors hovered above lawns, lit and frosted. Behind the glass, distorted figures took off their shoes.

"It looks beautiful," said Kalgrash.

"Except," said Gregory, "if I may repeat myself, sunset equals death."

"Oh," said Kalgrash bashfully. "Death. I forgot."

Brian said, "Somehow I'll feel safer once we're in the caverns."

"Righto," said Kalgrash. "Under the mountain. We want to get to the mountain."

"Duh," said Gregory, somewhat unhelpfully.

"So it would probably be bad if we were back where we started." Kalgrash pointed. "At the house with the guy hiding in his floor."

There it was. Right down the street.

The boys stared in surprise.

141

Brian whispered, "We must have been turned around when we were at the center of the development. We ended up coming back sideways instead of going straight toward the mountain."

"These stupid roads," Gregory muttered. "They never go straight."

"We'll never make it out of the neighborhood by nightfall," said Brian.

"I wonder what Milton Deatley will send after us," said Kalgrash. "I hope it's not Gelt the Winnower."

Brian looked sharply at Kalgrash. They had never had to confront Gelt — just elude him. The idea of him drifting down the dark streets, the light from faux lanterns glistening on his mobile and restless silver cords, was terrifying.

"We've got to get back to Prudence's house," said Brian. "We have to prepare ourselves for a siege. We only have forty-five minutes or so left."

"We don't know it will be Gelt the Winnower," said Kalgrash. "There are plenty of other abominations in the area. It's a good neighborhood for abominations."

Brian didn't respond. He said, "Come on," and charged off in the direction of Prudence's home.

"Who made you boss?" Gregory grumbled, but he followed.

The three of them scurried through darkening streets. No longer were the green trees gold and brass. Light thinned. The boys ran, and Kalgrash clanked behind them.

Windows stood out more clearly, lit against the

darkness, as if they had been cut out of some dark card. Houses were blue.

Gregory pointed. The sun was entirely behind the trees. The sky was sapped of color, getting pale. At the other end of heaven's dome, the moon rose.

The three turned the corner. The ranch house was at the end of the street. They rushed toward it.

Kids were on their bikes, circling at the crossroads. The children watched with hooded eyes.

"Heya," Gregory said, absently, passing.

One little boy said, "They're coming for you."

Another said, "They've left their dens."

A third said, "You should of runned."

And as Brian and Gregory turned, terrified, to see the little stark children speaking while riding, the kids sang. They sang a little ditty while Brian, Gregory, and Kalgrash went into Prudence's house.

"Red, orange, yellow, green.
Half of life remains unseen.
Blue, indigo, violet, white.
Truth is truth and sight is sight.
'Cause truth's still truth when you are dead
And have no eyeballs in your head.
So watch all things now fade with night
And know that nothing turns out right."

Inside, Kalgrash, Brian, and Gregory prepared the house for a siege.

143

TWENTY

The little ranch house had to withstand invasion. It could come from any direction, or from several directions at once.

Furniture in front of the windows was the first thing. Bookshelves slid across the rug, hopping on the pile. The boys pulled an old wooden trunk as a barrier across the base of the sliding glass doors. Brian stood for a moment afterward and looked into the night. Moisture had gotten between the panes of glass and they were frosted. Nothing but falling darkness could be seen outside.

Brian knew that anything could be out there waiting or heaving its way through the shadows. Hiding on the edge of lawns. Pulling back fronds to observe the house from afar. He pictured himself, a small lit figure, framed in a foggy window.

And somewhere out there: Prudence. Waiting for them. Needing help.

In the kitchen, he filled pots and pans with water and set them to boil. He planned to use them as weapons. The stove smelled of hot, rancid grease.

Kalgrash and Gregory raided the basement. There were bags of fertilizer, birdseed, and salt, which they could prop against windows. Gregory grabbed some tools and hung them on his belt.

"You know who I wish we had with us?" Gregory muttered. "Bob Barren, P.I. From television. He could make a cannon out of pepper and a trash can. Or a bomb out of Lysol."

Kalgrash picked up a snow tire under each arm. "Too bad he's not here," he agreed.

"For Bob Barren, P.I., home cleaning products are basically an arsenal. He once brought a drug cartel to its knees with a Swiffer."

"You're awfully cheerful," Kalgrash observed.

"The closer to death Bob Barren gets, the more jaunty his jokes." Gregory headed upstairs with his arms full of tools.

He and Kalgrash were nailing boards over the plate-glass window on the landing.

"There's only one actual weapon in this house," Gregory said, hammering.

"The blunderbuss," Brian said from up above.

"Yeah. We should check if it has bullets."

"Do you know how to fire a blunderbuss?" Brian asked. "Isn't it, like, a muzzle loader?"

"A 'muzzle loader'?" Gregory protested. "What are

you talking about? You fire a gun by going *BANG! BANG! BANG!* How difficult can it be?"

Brian went over to take the Norumbegan gun down from above the mantelpiece. He inspected it. "I wonder if you need gunpowder?"

It was at that moment his eye fell upon the plaque beneath the gun. It said,

NORUMBEGAN "Brown Bess" Musket
c. 220 B.E.

"This is it!" Brian exclaimed. "This is Prudence's friend Bess!"

"What is?" asked Gregory. The hammer was held in a casual backswing as he waited for an answer.

"The blunderbuss!" said Brian. "I completely remember this now from American history. They used to call their muskets brown besses."

"What? Who?"

"People in Colonial America."

"When?"

"You know. Back in the day."

"Why?"

Brian shrugged. "I don't know. You were in the same class."

"Yeah, but *I* wasn't paying attention."

"I think it was *Bess* from *blunderbuss*. Or from Elizabeth the First. The Queen of England."

146

"You remember too much."

"I don't remember enough. I don't know how to work this thing," said Brian, turning it over carefully in his hands.

Gregory was excited. "There must be bullets around." He stood. "Give it here. Let me check it out."

"Keep hammering, Kojak," grunted Kalgrash, holding a board in place.

"One sec," said Gregory, jogging up the steps to Brian's side. "Can you see how to work it? Let me see."

Brian was inspecting it. "I can't tell," he mumbled vaguely, turning it over again. "There's no . . ."

"Oh, come on! It's a gun! Just pull the trigger and —" He lifted it out of Brian's hands. "What's so tough?" He looked down its barrel.

"Careful," Brian warned. "Maybe she's already loaded it."

Gregory pointed it at a window. He sighted along the barrel.

"There's no trigger," he said.

"I know," Brian agreed. "I was just saying that."

"How are you supposed to work a gun without a trigger?"

"I don't know."

"That sucks. You might as well hold up a broom and go *bang bang*."

"She said —"

"There's got to be something on here."

"She said she would 'say the magic word.'"

"Which is what?"

Brian considered, frowning. "Oh, I bet —"

"There's something outside!" Kalgrash hissed.

The two boys looked, startled, at the front door. There was a stealthy scratching upon the wood.

"Battle positions," Kalgrash whispered.

Gregory padded back down to the landing. Something was trying to get in. Gregory picked up his hammer.

Kalgrash stood, retrieving his battle-ax from where he'd leaned it in the corner. Carefully, he bent back so he could see out the window. For a long moment, he stared.

"What?" Gregory demanded. "What is it?"

"A cat," said Kalgrash. "A kitten. No, cat. But petite."

"It must be Melior!" Brian said. "We need to put out some food for her. She's probably starving."

Kalgrash pointed out, "If you put out food for her, she'll stick around. She'll still be out there when the monsters get here."

"Let it in," said Gregory. "It's better off in here than out there."

"What if it's a trap?" said Brian.

"It's a cat." Gregory unlocked the locks and opened the door.

The cat, a small tiger-striped orange tabby, darted in and nosed around the bowl. There was nothing left.

"I let her out a few days ago," said Kalgrash. The cat rubbed against his greaves.

"You let that cat out?" said Brian.

"Yeah. Is anyone going to nail up the other end of this plank, or am I just squatting here holding it for the night?"

148

"And were there any other cats?" Brian asked. "In the house?"

Kalgrash said, "No. Come on, Gregory. Hammer. Hammer in the morning. Hammer in the evening. And all over this landing."

Gregory picked up a nail from a coffee can and rested the point on the board. He started to bang at it.

"Wait. Stop," said Brian.

The other two stopped.

"Because," Brian said, "the cat hair we've found all over the house is gray, not orange-striped."

Kalgrash's face paled. He dropped his eyes to the cat. It bolted downstairs.

"Grab it," said Brian. "Grab it! It might not be a cat!"

Gregory tossed the hammer to Kalgrash and bounded down the steps. They heard him bash his way through the storage room in the basement. "Here, kitty!" he called. "Stay cute! No mandibles! No tentacles!"

Brian put the blunderbuss on the sofa and ran down the stairs, past Kalgrash.

"There is another end of this plank," Kalgrash pointed out to no one. "I'm holding it up."

Brian looked briefly into the room where the Norumbegan symbols of protection had been lined up on the floor. He wondered whether —

"*Ow!*" Gregory yelped. "He scratched me! I almost had his head."

Brian rushed into the storage room. "You shouldn't try to pick her up by her head."

149

"Sorry. I forgot your degree in veterinary medicine."

"I'm just saying —"

"I think I can pick up a cat, thanks."

"Gregory, I'm sorry if I'm somehow . . ."

"You're not 'somehow.' Where'd he go?"

"She."

"See? Does it really matter? If he's a cat of evil?"

"Here's a cat box, for example. For cars and planes and stuff. If you hold the box, I'll grab —"

The cat slipped by behind Brian and thumped up the stairs.

The boys turned and ran after her, the carrying case flapping at Brian's side.

"I am kind of thinking," said Kalgrash, still kneeling, holding wood, "that the cat is not an avatar of evil. When the Thusser threaten someone, they mean more than just licking your knuckles with a raspy tongue. It tends to be more, you know, death, damnation, torture, et cetera."

The two boys were up the stairs. They split up — Brian heading for the kitchen and dining room, Gregory heading down the hall toward Prudence's bedroom.

Brian flicked on the light in the kitchen. The cat was sitting on the counter, nosing around the dirty dishes. The gray cat fur was plastered to plates, to knives, to forks, to spoons. The cat sniffed at it.

On the stove, several saucepans and spaghetti pots were on the boil. Their lids rattled.

Brian walked slowly toward the cat. "She's here," he called out. He held up the travel box.

The cat saw it and leaped, loping around the corner into the dining room.

Brian followed the cat, stepping quietly on the wall-to-wall carpet. He put the box down. He got down on his haunches and slid carefully forward. He held out his hand for the cat to sniff. "Come on, girl."

The cat, terrified by days of roaming through nightmare suburbs, did a small dancing step backward, then inched toward Brian's fingers. She pouted and stuck out her snout. The little petals of her nose fluttered near Brian's fingers.

And then some creature outside threw itself against the plate glass and began pounding.

TWENTY-ONE

A crash. Brian stood, swiveled.

A dark shape threw itself against the frosted sliding glass doors, raking at the handle.

"Gregory! Kalgrash!" Brian yelled.

There were two attackers now at the back door, bashing at it with their crystalline fists — two more like the monster the boys had broken in the street — fists hardening with every blow. *Kreslings*, Kalgrash had called them.

There was a hideous slam — and the door fractured. A hole had been punched out. A fist flew through and groped around while the creatures cackled.

Kalgrash was there with his battle-ax. "There's more coming across the lawn," he said.

He whacked with his ax. Nothing — the flesh firmed like granite. The ax couldn't slice. The beast fumbled for the lock as Kalgrash, screaming in irritation, hacked at the hardening skin.

Brian ran for the blunderbuss. There was something he wanted to try.

Gregory watched out Prudence's bedroom window as three more of the monsters, their vitreous flesh glittering, charged across the lawn.

One of these things had been bad enough, the night before. Now at least five had surrounded the house. The three on the front lawn leaped and hopped as they approached.

Gregory smiled.

There were cans and things for throwing stacked next to the desk, and he had a good arm. He hurled a Progresso soup and beaned a monster, but its flesh gathered quickly. The can dented and fell on the grass. The monster did, too — Gregory had aimed at a knee, trying to lock it up firm just long enough to trip the thing. The monster fell for an instant. Gregory yelled, "Ha!" out the window. But the monster was quickly pliable. It rose and charged again.

Throwing things would do no good. Gregory grabbed some gear and ran for the front door.

Kalgrash was slowing up the invasion through the back door by chipping away at the fumbling hand. He couldn't make a dent in the rippled flesh, but he could slow the thing down by hardening it so frequently that its fingers became stiff and immobile. He battered relentlessly, glad the one kresling blocked the other.

There were three coming for Gregory and the front door. He and Kalgrash hadn't finished nailing planks over the window on the landing. All it would take was one kick to the plate glass, and the monsters would be inside the house.

153

Gregory, with a mingled fear and a weird joy in battle, raised up a contraption he'd rigged out of a bottle of kitchen cleaner and a lighter.

The monsters were at the door. They were bashing at it — then leering in through the window — reaching up with one heavy fist and whacking. The glass went flying. Gregory, on the stairs, shielded his face.

The monster in front was knocking at the planks, trying to dislodge them so it could step in. It climbed one rung, stepped back, wiggled the wood.

Gregory raised his contraption and declared, "When the action gets hot, the hot get active!" — Bob Barren, P.I.'s, slogan, declaimed when he jumped from copters into resort pools filled with nitroglycerine. Gregory jabbed his thumb down on the aerosol button and started spraying. He lit the spray.

For an instant, he was jubilant. It was just like on TV.

A huge blast of flame. The monsters were thrown back.

Then Gregory realized that his own hand was singed.

He screamed, dropped everything on the tile floor — just as the monsters were peeking past the smoldering planks.

"Curse you, Bob Barren!" Gregory roared, slamming the hand again and again on the wall in absolute agony.

In the back of the house, a kresling thumb flipped a catch. The sliding doors were unlocked. The kresling began to work them open.

Kalgrash's mighty, mailed hand seized the handle and dragged the door back into place. The glass jags sliced at the monster's trapped arm — causing it, once again, to calcify or get cut. Hard as a gem, the arm was jammed in the fractured hole.

The kresling screamed with rage and dragged at the door, trying to force it open. Kalgrash ground his teeth and held the door closed.

Another fist slammed the glass. Twice: once to harden, a second time to punch through. Then another hand was fumbling for Kalgrash's neck.

He backed up.

The kreslings tripped — fell — and the door finally slid open.

They rose, gruesome mouths working.

Kalgrash skittered sideways into the kitchen, picked up one of the spaghetti pots from the stove, and threw the boiling water at his enemies.

They screamed — one cracked — his face popped like glass and splintered — he fell — and the other, howling with anger, crawled over his body to do battle with the troll.

On the landing, Gregory looked up from the unbearable pain of his burned hand. The monsters were pulling off the few planks still blocking the broken plate-glass window.

With his other hand, Gregory picked up the hammer from the floor.

He hurled it.

He was not surprised when it smacked the monster in the head and dropped without effect. The head had hardened.

The charred wood went scattering down the stairs.

The first monster lumbered into the house.

Gregory cowered, screamed.

It reached for him.

And Brian, at the top of the stairs, holding the blunderbuss, cast the Cantrip of Activation.

A blast of light.

The monster stumbled back, its chest a shard-lined pit of blue flame. It was dead.

The next one was already inside. Brian called out the word again, and again the muzzle blasted magic flame.

Gregory looked on in awe.

Kalgrash and a creature clashed in the kitchen, armor and hard flesh grating and rattling. The huge ax clanged again and again on the dense hide.

The monster swiped, caught his claw on Kalgrash's steel faulds, and yanked.

Kalgrash reached out for a boiling saucepan with one hand as he swung his ax with the other.

No dice. He had the handle, but the pot tipped — and most of the hot liquid spilled.

The monster dragged him down.

Kalgrash slammed the boiling pot against the thing's head and — while the flesh up there was still bunched up and hard — buried the hatchet in the monster's lower back, enclosing him almost in an embrace. The thing cried out, flopped over liquidly, and pooled.

Two down. More already in the door.

And then he heard something in the hall. Something had climbed in the bathroom window. It was headed his way.

156

At the front door, Brian was holding the monsters at bay. They wouldn't come through, having seen the first two dispatched by Old Bess. Several of them loitered by the stoop, waiting for a chance to invade. They knew, clearly, that two of them could take Brian out before he could fire twice — but one of them would die in the process.

"We need to be in a more secure position," Brian shouted. He thought quickly.

Something was headed down the hallway. Brian looked and saw a different horror — a collection of gray stumps fumbling toward him — something like a ball of truncations, wrinkled flesh, padding down the carpeted corridor.

Brian had a choice. Stumps or vitreous humanoid. One or the other would get by him.

He called out, "Kalgrash!" and, keeping the blunderbuss trained on the monsters outside the door, started to make his way down the debris-littered stairs. "Come on, Gregory," he said.

Gregory was only half sitting up. He kept wringing his hand in the air. He looked, confused, at Brian.

The stump beast made it to the top of the stairs and flexed to throw itself on Brian's head.

Brian knew that if he took the gun away from the monsters at the door for one second, they'd be inside, gouging Gregory and him.

Gregory slid to his knees and tried to rise. The monsters outside were gloating and waiting for their chance.

The stumpy ball prepared to knock Brian down.

157

And then Kalgrash's ax buried itself deep in the gray, elephantine flesh. Kalgrash gave a whooping battle roar.

"Kalgrash!" Brian yelled. "We're going down to the safe room! With the symbols! It's more defendable!"

"Says who?" Gregory demanded.

"It's one door," said Kalgrash. He bustled down the stairs. "I don't know who thought of these open-plan houses. Awful for siege warfare."

Brian put his hand down to help Gregory up.

"I can get up myself," Gregory complained.

"Well," said Brian, eying the monsters outside the door warily, "then —"

"Since when did you get so bossy?"

"Since you're just sitting there on the floor, Gregory!"

"With a burned hand! From my Bob Barren trick! It turns out that a little old-fashioned ingenuity doesn't go a long way."

"So come on and —"

The monsters charged Brian. He raised the blunderbuss, fumbled the spell (surprised, unthinking), and the gun didn't go off. Gregory fell down the steps. Kalgrash couldn't swing his ax with Brian in the way.

The monsters pawed at Brian's arm. He cast the Cantrip again. The gun discharged. There was a blast.

One had been beheaded, and sifted into grayish dust. The other still kicked at glass and tried to pull off Brian's limbs.

Kalgrash hit the thing with a solid blow.

It did no good. The blow just locked the monster's grip around Brian's arm, solid as marble.

158

Brian twisted the gun to get the muzzle pointing at the monster's head.

Gregory was limping down the final steps.

Kalgrash hit the thing again, Brian shouted his Cantrip, and the gun blew the thing apart.

The three ran for the room in the basement.

They swooped in, careful not to disturb the amulets lying in rows on the floor. Brian stood by the open door. "Kalgrash, you watch the window."

The window had a sack of driveway salt crammed into it.

Kalgrash stood there at the ready.

Brian concentrated on thinking the Cantrip, so he would be able to fire in an instant if something appeared by the door to the protected chamber.

There was no sound in the house. Everything that had attacked them so far was destroyed. All three listened carefully. No movement. No thumps in the halls. No heavy breathing of ugly maws on the landing.

In the distance, at the crossroads, there was the singing of the children on their bikes, riding in their circles. They sang that nothing would come out right.

"We should get those kids," said Gregory.

Brian shook his head. "I think they're safe."

"They're out there playing Duck, Duck, Goose with baby-killing ogres from another dimension."

"I think the Thusser are using those kids to spy on us. I think the Thusser can see everything those kids see. That's why that ring of kids is posted there. The Thusser aren't going to hurt them."

Gregory flapped his hand, trying to shake off the pain. "You always have to be the one to figure things out, don't you?" he accused Brian. "Maybe I'm right for once."

Brian was tired and anxious. He demanded, "Why are you being like this?"

"See?" Gregory said. "You wouldn't have ever yelled at me before. Back — a year ago."

Kalgrash said, reasonably, "But you're being a jerk."

Gregory retorted, "Says who?" And to Brian: "Just because you know a few spells, you've become completely bossy."

"It just seems like this room might be the best place to be if there's another round of something attacking us."

"We can't leave little children riding their bikes out there."

"They're as safe out there as they'll be near us," said Kalgrash.

"So you're just going to let them ride around out there?" said Gregory. "Alone? With the monsters?"

Brian thought about it. He really did believe the kids were safe for the moment, but he didn't want Gregory to feel like no one listened to him. "Okay," he said. "So what do you want to do?"

"I'll lead an expedition out," said Gregory.

"Who's your expedition?" Kalgrash asked.

Gregory thought about it. He looked from Brian to Kalgrash.

"All three of us," he said.

Brian said, "So we'll go out and get the kids to come in here with us?"

"Right. So they're safe."

Kalgrash said, "You want the Thusser listening in to our every word?"

"I want to save the kids."

"No. You want to be the one shouting orders and with us all admiring you and your hair."

Gregory said, "A kresling tried to grab a little boy the other night."

"He's right," said Brian. "They did try to take one of the kids."

Gregory said triumphantly, "See?"

Kalgrash closed his eyes, exhaled, and nodded.

So, carefully, they left the room with its sigils on the floor.

They went out into the hallway.

No sooner had they stepped out of the safe room than they smelled something awful. Cat urine. Overpowering. A high, searing reek.

Kalgrash sniffed. "What is that?"

"Let's go," said Gregory, forging forward.

"Look!" Brian said, pointing at the walls.

The walls were growing hair. The nap of the rug was growing hair. The ceiling was growing hair.

The three of them ran for the stairs.

The stairs were covered in gray shag. It was waving. The three coughed with dander.

There was no door, no window. They were vined and wound with fur.

The walls now waved with long tendrils of gray hair. Brian's shoes were entangled in the extrusions of the rug.

161

Everything was fur. They were inside something. The house itself had become animal.

The floor shuddered.

Kalgrash yelped.

"Back to the safe room!" Brian screamed. He pointed back to where he could see the clean rug, the neat rows of protective signs.

"Let's try to get out!" Gregory said. "Kalgrash can cut through fur."

"Something's wrong," Kalgrash said, pointing at the floor.

The floor trembled, then dropped.

The boys screamed. The house was tilting.

Or a pit was opening up.

Or a gullet.

Brian scrambled back into the safe room. He tottered on the threshold.

He looked behind him and saw the whole of the house resolving into one long, furry throat. It was trying to swallow them whole.

And suddenly, he knew this was what had happened to Prudence. She had been writing that e-mail, trying to warn them, telling them she'd be fleeing the suburb, coming down to Boston the next day. And as she typed, she had not noticed, in the shadows of her room, the fronds of hair growing. She had not noticed the prickly growths in the corners, the long mane hanging off the goose-necked lamp.

She had not noticed until she looked up and found herself in the midst of the monster, swallowed whole.

The room in which Brian stood, surrounded by army ranks of protective signs, was still stable. It was rectilinear. Outside, everything was soft and yielding and the floor sloped away toward someplace underground.

Kalgrash and Gregory were slipping and stumbling toward the safe room.

Brian seized hold of the doorjamb and extended a hand. "Come on!" he yelled. "Come on!"

The house convulsed.

Gregory screamed, fell over. He grabbed at the fur. Kalgrash gave a fierce yell and buried his ax in the wall. That gave him purchase — he reached out a hand. He tried to grab Gregory's.

"That's my burned — ouch!" Gregory yanked his hand away.

Below him now snaked a hairy throat. A straight drop.

He looked down — he paled. He held out his other hand.

Kalgrash, closer, reached for the fingers that quivered there. Just a few more inches. A few more.

Kalgrash edged out, trembling, suspended on the slope by the haft of his ax.

He reached out his mailed claw. His fingers were touching Gregory's.

Almost there.

Almost.

The house convulsed again.

Gregory shrieked and, with his good hand, grabbed at the fur to hold himself up. The other was too badly burned. The fingers couldn't close. They couldn't clutch.

"Give me your hand," rasped Kalgrash. "Come on."

"I can't," said Gregory. "I can't let go."

"Your other hand. Your bad hand."

"It's burned."

"I know. Give it —"

A tuft of hair, with the sound of grass pulled up, uprooted.

And Gregory, suspended by those hairs, fell.

He dropped into the hole.

Brian screamed.

Gregory tumbled.

Kalgrash reached his arm after the boy.

But Gregory was gone.

TWENTY-TWO

Mrs. Drake turned off the television. It was time for bed. Her husband was already upstairs, reading a magazine. Mrs. Drake got up from the couch and crinkled up the remains of a bag of corn chips. She threw it in the trash and headed for the stairs.

She couldn't believe she had just wasted an evening. A perfectly beautiful evening. The shows on TV were getting stupider and stupider, she thought to herself. Recently, they had just been rooms full of men with dark-ringed eyes and pointed ears sitting around, staring at the camera. They didn't speak. They seemed to be waiting for something, which was why, she guessed, she kept watching. You never knew when something might change or arrive.

She stopped on the stairs. She wanted to step outside. It was too beautiful an evening to have spent it inside on the couch. The air through the window screens smelled of summer and green and youth.

She padded down the steps and opened the front

door. She went out into the cool of the night. She wrapped her arms around herself and admired the peace of it all.

There were a few lights on at the ends of driveways. They were embedded in stone pillars or were crafted to look like old-time lanterns.

The first few crickets were starting to sing. In another few weeks, the night would be full of them. The houses all looked slumberous. The kids at the crossroads no longer wheeled on their bikes. They were silent, standing in a circle, their bicycles held upright in their hands. They were all staring at that ticky-tacky 1960s ranch-style house at the end of the street.

She wondered, in passing, why her own children were in the street, perched on a tricycle and a Big Wheel, when they should be in bed. She did not think she had given anyone permission.

Her brow creased; and then, suddenly, she blinked and smiled. She had recalled, in a rush, her childhood in Ohio: learning how to ride her bike with training wheels. Her father taught her, jogging alongside her. He would say, "That's a girl!" She had pretended to be clumsier than she really was; she had pretended that she couldn't stop the bike from tipping, just so her father would stay by her side, praising her, teaching her, holding her shoulder, and they wouldn't have to go in.

And now her own kids were there, outside, in a ring, at midnight, staring.

With shock, Mrs. Drake saw that the windows of the

ranch house were broken and the front door was open. Something had happened there.

There was something awful about that little house. Something hideous in the jagged glass, the singed planks sagging in the window. Mrs. Drake, suddenly, was terrified.

The kids should not be out.

She called their names. "Cassie! Charlton!"

All the kids in the circle turned. They all looked at her. Their faces were pale.

There was no moon. Just stars.

And the children of the neighborhood — Charlton, Cassie, and all their little friends — stared at her, as if to say, "Now we see you. You're next."

✳ ✳ ✳

Brian kept screaming Gregory's name even as the hair in the house receded, even as the floor became solid and the rugs shed their fur.

There were wisps of hair everywhere.

Brian was down on his hands and knees, paddling at the cement. There was no give. No sign that Gregory had ever stood there next to them. Gray fur eddied through the hallway.

Kalgrash was stationed with his back to the wall, battle-ax raised, awaiting some new monstrosity.

"He's gone," said Brian. "They've taken him."

Kalgrash nodded vaguely.

167

"We have to find him!" Brian demanded.

"Some people really benefit from being held prisoner," Kalgrash said. "They learn a lot of important lessons about friendship."

Brian scowled.

"And survival," Kalgrash continued, sighing. "And rescuing."

"We've got to get down there. Down to the castle."

Kalgrash nodded.

"Let's go," said Brian.

Surrounded by shards of glass and kresling, they raided the kitchen for crackers and cheese to eat while they walked. Brian hadn't eaten for many hours. He went to Prudence's room and picked up the magical lantern he and Gregory had been using for light in the room. He held it in one hand and hung the blunderbuss on its strap across his shoulder. Then he and Kalgrash sneaked out the back door. They knew the kids were watching the front. If the Thusser could indeed see through the eyes of the children, then they'd have to avoid the gaze of the tricycle circle.

Silently, they eased themselves over the barricade in front of the sliding doors. They made their way across the lawn.

"Toward the mountain," whispered Kalgrash.

Brian squinted. "Where is it?"

Kalgrash pointed with one mailed hand. His night vision was excellent.

"Not on the roads," Brian said. "They'll only lead us in circles. We just have to cut straight across."

Kalgrash nodded, clinking.

They headed up a rise. The previous year, it had been wooded, Brian thought — very steep — covered in old leaves. Now it was the lawn for a mansion. They carefully crawled up the slope.

They passed through someone's garden and came out on another street. This one didn't go very far before it dead-ended in a circle around a huge stone monolith: the Crooked Steeple.

It rose up, uneven and pitted, from shrubs. Brian recalled finding it with Kalgrash the previous fall. It was comforting to see something that reminded Brian of what the wood had been like. He was sure now that there hadn't been any houses around it, except for Prudence's. He was absolutely sure.

They slunk past the Steeple, intent on the mountain above the blue trees.

Through yards and along drainage ditches they ran, bent over, trying to stay out of sight.

That night, there was a feeling of youth in the air in Rumbling Elk Haven. The shadows were wet with life and growth; the trees looked young and spindly. The new suburb was silent except for the distant grinding of earth-movers, the chirp of crickets and of trucks in reverse, unseen, at the perimeter of the neighborhood, where work was being done even in darkness: the flattening of the forest, the raising of new homes, the spreading of settlement upon the face of the Earth in all directions, the ceaseless devouring.

Even as they ran, stooped, past pools, the neighborhood grew. The dominion of humankind shrank.

169

They came to a region of mud, steep and sticky. No one had built above this line. They toiled through it. Kalgrash had a hard time in his armor. The weight of it pulled him down.

"Look!" Kalgrash exclaimed. "Suckers!"

Brian thought he was sneering, but discovered instead that Kalgrash was embracing young trees.

"It's the forest!" he said. "They haven't knocked it down yet up here!"

"I think the trees that were originally in the forest were bigger than that," Brian said. "Weren't they full size?" He couldn't really remember.

"But these are darling!" said Kalgrash.

They climbed over boulders and through bracken. They followed old paths through the rocks on the mountain's side. Brian couldn't see well. There was hardly any moon. Kalgrash led him, sometimes heaving him up rock walls.

And after an hour, they reached the entrance to the caverns.

It was in a cellar. A rotten door set in the stone.

"I remember it being a foundation to a new house," said Brian.

He looked out over the landscape. Beneath the sliver of the moon and the high clouds, the suburb lay like an organism, glistening with lights, its streets curved and curled. An SUV crawled along one dead end. The lights peppered the wood as far as Brian could see.

That was just like he remembered it from the previous year, he thought. The lawns. The lanterns. The dead ends. Was that right?

170

He stood, transfixed by the distant, bruising glow of cities on the horizon. The clouds were dingy with their light.

The night was crawling with life.

Kalgrash, below, was heaving the wooden door aside.

"I'll go a few steps down," he said. "Then once we can't be seen, you light the lantern for yourself."

They trotted down the spiral staircase. Brian shrugged the sagging door closed over his head. Now in complete darkness, he held on to the lantern, concentrated, and spoke the Cantrip of Activation.

The lantern glowed and picked out Brian's round cheeks and Kalgrash's spiky teeth.

They continued downward, toward the city — and the prison where Gregory, Prudence, and Sniggleping were trapped, far beneath the earth.

TWENTY-THREE

When Gregory tumbled out of the hirsute throat of wizardry, he dropped on a floor of stone. The fall was rough. For a while, he lay on the ground, writhing, grabbing at his own arms, flexing his burned hand, rocking back and forth, convulsed in pain.

A Norumbegan lantern lit the dungeon, but not well. The room was too large, the shadows tremendous. Dark bars were cast across his scalded palm.

As he stopped rolling and began to take notice of what was around him, terror struck. He was surrounded by kreslings.

They stood without moving. He propped himself up. "What do you want?" he asked them.

Two came forward roughly, jammed their claws under his arms, and pulled him to his feet. Their flesh smelled of burning tires. They dragged him to the wall.

Then he was truly terrified.

Because there, in front of him, was Prudence.

He had wanted to find her so badly.

But not like this.

Nothing like this.

His cousin was already slumped on the floor, hands behind her. She could not see him. She had on some kind of helmet. On its crest was a small, old-timey movie projector. In front of her eyes were long tracks leading to some kind of screen, which caught the image from the projector above. The projector rattled and ratcheted. Gregory could not see the movie Prudence watched, but it obviously blared colors, which shrank and grew and dissolved across her forehead and eyes. As they changed, she twitched and grimaced. Her mouth was pulled into ugly shapes. She did not seem like a sentient human anymore, but like something that was broken.

Wee Sniggleping was next to her. He also wore a helmet with a projector and a screen a few inches in front of his eyes. He no longer moved. He stared, vainly, at the screen, his mouth open, his hands unclasped on the stone beside him.

"What have you — what is this?" Gregory asked.

The kreslings did not answer.

He called out Prudence's name. She did not respond. He called it out again.

She turned jerkily, trying to see him. But she could not see past the movie. She raised a hand to try to feel him. Her body jolted with the darts of color that assaulted her.

He was horrified this could happen to her — his clever, sly cousin — but now, there were no Rules to stop the wrong from winning — and here she lay, hardly human.

173

Gregory reached out to her with both his hands. One was red, one pale. He called her name again.

The kreslings forced him down to the ground. They tried to shove a helmet on his head. He fought them. He brought his elbows up to shield his skull. They batted his arms away. He clenched a fist and ducked.

They got the helmet on him regardless.

He shrieked Prudence's name again, but he couldn't see her anymore. There was only a white screen in front of him.

He did not have to ask. He knew what this was. Brainwashing. Somehow, they'd try to get him to soften up for colonization. There was no way, he vowed — no way that they'd break him.

He felt a *click* resound through his jaw. Someone had turned on the helmet's movie projector, and it wouldn't, he had a feeling, go off soon.

The colors started. Bold. Flying at him. He ducked. It was like they were three-dimensional. He knew they weren't real. He closed his eyes.

The machine purred on his head. He saw the colors through his lids — just a blush.

It seemed like more trouble to keep his eyes closed than to open them. He peeked.

The colors came at him in a barrage. Some subtle. Most glaring. Swimming up at him. He tried to wipe them away, but his hands were restrained by claws. He could not reach his own face. The colors were always there. The colors always would be there. For hours, for days, he would watch the colors. They crowded out every thought.

He screamed, but he couldn't hear his own voice above the nattering of the projector.

He tried to fix his thoughts on the things he knew — on home — on his mother, his father, his house. He saw the house, the kitchen, with an arrangement of dried grasses in a vase on the counter. A calendar of Vermont landscapes covered by fog — covered bridges, pony teams, valleys. The dishwasher . . . (everything turned purple before his eyes) . . . the dishwasher had a different compartment for powdered soap than for liquid. His father was there, putting away plates. Gregory thought as hard as possible about that room — the place he knew so well — with the cabinets and the arrangement of dried grass and the men with the dark rings around their eyes, the pointed ears, sitting on the tabletop. There was never a hope for brownies in that house. The Thusser ate them all. The walls were orange — no, yellow, or . . . with a green stripe . . . the walls . . . weren't the walls . . . ?

Gregory's head rocked back and forth as the colors assaulted him.

He lay on the floor, deep in that vault, and forgot everything he knew.

TWENTY-FOUR

The stairs curled around themselves forever. Centuries before, they'd connected a turret, a mountain outpost, with the maze of caverns beneath. Norumbegan soldiers had rushed up and down these steps during the Wars of Thusserian Aggression. Their halberds had clanged on the stone.

Down these stairs, in this late, unmythical age, a boy in glasses and a troll dressed for a joust descended into silence. As they passed farther and farther into the mountain, the chill grew. The summer's warmth never penetrated here.

At the bottom of the stairs, Brian hesitated. They were coming out into Snarth's Cavern, where, the previous fall, a blind ogre had stomped and raged and nearly flattened Brian and Gregory both.

Kalgrash poked around the cavern first, knees akimbo, ax ready for smiting.

He found that Snarth the blind ogre was long deactivated. He sat in a pile, head sagging between his warty knees. His mechanism had run down. He had not been wound for months.

This calmed Brian down a lot. They crossed the cavern, Brian shining his lantern to pick out stalactites and stalagmites, the mucilaginous flow of rock around which Snarth had nosed his way in former days.

"You know," said Kalgrash apologetically, "you're going to have to switch off the lantern."

"Why?" Brian asked.

"Because once we get into the cavern with the City of Gargoyles, the light will alert things that we're there. Whatever is waiting for us. And then it's nothing but claws, tentacles, tentacles, claws, teeth, spines, acid spouts, whiskers, cleavers, katanas, shillelaghs . . ."

"Okay," said Brian, "but how am I going to see?"

". . . fireous breath, razor-sharp dorsal plates, cat-o'-nine-tails — you get my drift." Kalgrash sputtered with his lips.

"I won't be able to see."

"But I'll be able to see better in total darkness than with your lamp. I'm a troll. Or at least, a good fake of one. And we won't get munged by anything with scales that happens to slither by."

"You'll have to guide me."

"Even better," said Kalgrash. "You sit on my shoulders. Holding up the blunderbuss. Then: *Clank. Clank. Clank.* We progress into the City of Gargoyles. We'll be like a tank. Medieval tank."

Brian extinguished the lantern with a Cantrip of Deactivation. Kalgrash lowered himself to one knee, and

177

Brian clambered on his shoulders. The arrangement required the dismantling of some of Kalgrash's armor. There were too many spikes on it.

So it was that they came to the vast arch that looked out over the City of Gargoyles.

Kalgrash could not see with complete precision in the total darkness, but he could certainly make out the city streets and the dark bay. At the head of the grandest avenue of the city rose the spires of the cathedral and, next to it, the Palace of the Norumbegans. It was in that palace that the prison cells lay. They had been abandoned by Norumbega ages ago, and now, Brian guessed, were being put to use by their adversaries.

"We have to make it the whole length of the city," Kalgrash said.

Brian stared into the gloom. "Do you see anything unusual? That shouldn't be there?"

"I can't make them out exactly. I see the sacs on the city streets. They look gray and very big. I bet they're Thusser luxury homes." He scanned the horizon. Brian could feel the troll's head swivel. "And there's . . . there's someone moving . . . up above the grand boulevard . . . someone . . . I can't really see from this distance. It's a little man."

"What's he doing?"

"Floating. Or hovering. I guess he shouldn't be doing that. Gravity's not just a good idea — it's the law."

"Do you think you can get us to the castle without going past him on the boulevard?"

"Side streets, hmm? We'll give it a shot."

Brian could not judge their progress. It seemed to take forever. They did not speak as the troll advanced, rocking, beneath him. Brian felt each jolt through his legs. He held the blunderbuss in readiness, but could see nothing to aim at.

He could hear, by the faint jingle and clank of the troll's armor, that they passed through wide spaces and narrow. He felt them trudge up steps and down through sunken channels.

The darkness was claustrophobic or frightening, even though there was nothing pressing down on him, nothing closing him in. There was just the vastness of blank space and chill around him. He couldn't tell if there was nothing above his head for five hundred feet, or if a stone beam or lintel was about to bash him senseless.

He found himself ducking instinctively to try to avoid hazards that weren't even there.

He wished Gregory were there to make a joke about his blindness.

Suddenly, Kalgrash jerked sideways. He slammed backward into a stone wall. Brian fumbled to keep hold of the blunderbuss.

"What is it?" the boy croaked.

Kalgrash moved swiftly backward. Then to the side. Brian couldn't tell what was going on.

"Can't even close its mouth," said Kalgrash.

Brian heard something approach. Claws on stone.

Kalgrash said, "Ready!" He reached up, grabbed the tip of the blunderbuss, and aimed it into the darkness.

179

A jolt — Kalgrash had been hit. He rocked backward, stumbled to keep his balance with the boy on top of him.

He cried, *"Fire!"*

And Brian cast the Cantrip of Activation.

Flare bloomed.

In the brief shock of fire, Brian saw something lizard-like and vicious, maw so wide and so deeply fanged it drooped open. It burned.

Kalgrash began running.

Brian asked, "Are there more of them?" At each step, he juddered up and down, slapping against the troll's spaulders.

"No," said the troll. "Worse. The light of the blast."

"Who saw?"

"That floating guy. He saw."

"How do you know?"

"I can see him over the roofs."

"Flying?"

"No. I think it's little cords. It's Gelt the Winnower. He's headed this way."

TWENTY-FIVE

Suspended above the boulevards, suspended, too, between life and death, Gelt the Winnower, once a man (or something like one), now a monster, patrolled the dark spaces beneath the mountain for his Thusser masters. The cords erupting from his hands, his legs, his chest, his eyes, all gently lofted him through the cold subterranean air. They caressed the smoothness of marble, the rough heft of granite. He felt the cold stone all around him, and pulled himself along in utter gloom.

Dimly, he could recall life lived upon his own feet — another world — much more noise, more glow, delightful color (for others, never for him). People leaned together at cafés and in homes, and he remembered attachments to people who called him by another name. He did not regret that he had chosen a strange and wayward route to power. He wanted only to destroy more effectively, and here he hung, feared by all.

His thoughts — husky in his brittle, dried head — were limited to the routes he'd followed in the last twelve hours, surveying the dead city to ensure that none of its former citizens, alerted, had returned. He had wound himself a cocoon, a spiral web, of his own silver cords, perched atop the peak of a conical turret on a defunct banker's house; he'd hung there for fifteen minutes, filaments twitching around him, searching for movement.

And then — there was light.

A burst: a gun.

Without sound, rapid as a cat, Gelt unwound himself. He drew himself silently along rooftops, up shingled planes, down gutters, through alleys, chin forward, eyes bristling with strands. In his dead heart was the joy of the hunt and the desire, after the chase, for embrace — to clutch his enemy tight, tighter, until the cords cut and the flesh failed and he was left alone again in silence.

He rushed to meet his adversary.

❋ ❋ ❋

Kalgrash bounded through the deserted alleyways. They had no light to give them away, true, but Brian could tell what a clatter the armor made. He was sure it echoed loudly above the silent city. Gelt would be upon them in moments.

Now the darkness filled Brian with panic. It was as if the ink in the air were a substance, something he breathed into his lungs with the chill, and he was sunk deep in some sea. He did not know from which way the cord would come, plucking at him, garroting him as Kalgrash thumped on, unawares.

182

He just wanted it to happen, to be over with, because he could not stand knowing that the danger was all around him and invisible, the fibers waiting to strike.

Brian's arm knocked against the wall of a house. It stung. He swayed on the troll's back. He gathered himself and hissed, "Inside!"

Kalgrash nodded, made an abrupt turn.

The space was close. Brian could tell from the echoes. Down a flight of stairs.

Deep in his nostrils, the scent of dust.

"Get down! *Get down!*" Kalgrash demanded. He lowered himself to one knee. Brian scrambled off.

Kalgrash pushed Brian down more steps. The troll half held him, half shoved him. Brian shuffled on the stone, barking his shins, slamming his hands into granite walls.

They were in some deep, small place. A cellar, maybe.

"Sit," Kalgrash demanded.

The two of them crouched on a dirt floor, their backs against frigid stone.

They tried to calm their breathing. Their mouths were open. They tried for silence.

For a minute, the air was as empty of sound as it was of image. Brian had only the sensation of rock in his back to mire him in the world of objects. Otherwise, there was nothing to suggest a world was there at all.

And then, a sound came. A stealthy ticking.

Gelt was above the house. His tendrils looped and curled down through its windows, under its lintels and across its floors. They crept along, feeling for humankind.

Brian could barely breathe with panic.

183

He heard the cords making their way through rooms.

Kalgrash whispered, "This isn't going to work. Hiding here."

Brian didn't want to respond. He didn't want to say anything, and to have that hushed word be the thing that got them caught.

Kalgrash said, "I'll lead the Winnower away and come back."

Brian had already lost Gregory. He couldn't lose Kalgrash. Chest pounding, he tried not to breathe. He could hear the tendrils licking the house, tapping through each room.

"I'm going," said Kalgrash.

"You can't do that," Brian insisted.

Then Kalgrash lunged. He stood. "Stay where you are. Exactly," the troll demanded, and leaped up the steps.

Brian sat absolutely still and waited for the troll to come back, or the Winnower to find him.

✳ ✳ ✳

Kalgrash saw the cords draped through the windows and doors, looping through rooms.

He ran past them, heading for the exit.

Feeling the percussion of armor on stone, Gelt's cords twitched and sought the troll harder. His servant fronds hopped and scurried through the house. Kalgrash leaped over them.

He jumped through a window and started bolting down the alley.

184

He saw, above him, the hideous, mangled form of Gelt. The slack, white body hung in the air, supported by the silver cords that now whipped out of windows and reached for the troll.

Kalgrash wanted to make it a few blocks away before he was caught. He wanted to give Brian as much space as possible.

A cord brushed his shoulder. He leaped into a house.

The tendrils poured in after him.

Kalgrash was already lumbering down a corridor, breathing heavily, looking for another — preferably confusing — way out.

The tendrils turned all corners at once.

Kalgrash put a heavy foot on the stone sill of a window and prepared to heave himself out.

A cord tapped, confirmed — then grabbed.

It was around his neck. He was astonished that something so gentle, so pliable, could suddenly snap taut and kill.

There were plates on his helm that protected his neck — but he could feel them creaking on their staples. He was trapped, half in, half out the window.

With a jerk, the cord pulled him up off his feet.

And others were there now to join in the fun. They crawled all over him. He struggled, stranded in a window.

✳ ✳ ✳

Brian sat motionless in the basement. He did not hear the Winnower any longer. Still, he wasn't going to move.

185

The darkness was total. Brian didn't want to think how far he was beneath the earth. There was a mountain on top of him. Enough dirt and rock to fill his mouth and nose and pack his throat solid fifty thousand times over.

He had lost Gregory. He couldn't imagine it. It felt impossible, that Gregory wasn't here, wisecracking. Brian tried to imagine what Gregory would say if he were there. He himself couldn't think of anything funny.

Brian couldn't believe how badly this whole mission had gone. They never would have even known where Prudence was if they hadn't run into Kalgrash. And now Kalgrash was gone, too. And families were still being absorbed into their houses. And the Thusser settlement was spreading.

And here he was, trapped in a cellar of a ruined house deep beneath a mountain, with a nightmare plucking at the air around him to try to find him —

Where was Kalgrash? Why wasn't he back yet?

And then, out of the darkness, Brian heard a voice. It was someone in the house above him. Someone was hissing, "Brian. Brian."

It sounded like Kalgrash. But Brian couldn't hear for sure.

"Come on," whispered Kalgrash, above him. Kalgrash, who had said to stay put regardless.

"Come on, Brian."

Uncertain, blind, Brian began slowly to climb the steps on his hands and knees.

Toward the voice.

TWENTY-SIX

Kalgrash, suspended, screamed, *"I SHALL SMITE!"* — which he thought was really very impressive, very epic poem, very chain-mail-and-broadsword — and swung his ax as hard as he could.

Several cords snapped, and Kalgrash toppled backward through the window. Several more cords snapped with the sudden shift of his weight.

Wham! He hit the soil in a long-dead courtyard. His breath was taken away. For a minute, he couldn't move. The tendrils were already slithering through the window to fetch him again.

He imagined how many bodies had hung from these willowlike fronds. How many bodies had dangled beneath the Winnower. Gelt was a human gallows.

Kalgrash, panicky, dragged himself across cobblestones.

Gelt's cords were retracting so he could reach the troll more directly, without having to detour through the mansion.

A great opportunity, thought Kalgrash, to live and smite another day.

He charged across the courtyard, skirting the lip of a dry old impluvium frilled with lichen.

His ax! Nicked!

It was almost out of his hand when he seized it harder. The cords were all around him.

He turned his head fearfully and saw, through his visor, Gelt suspended just a few feet above the dead mounds of the garden, grinning.

The troll bounded into a colonnade. The tendrils followed.

Kalgrash ran slalom. He weaved back and forth between the columns. Gelt's hideous cords followed, rearing back, jetting forward, seizing upon a shin or an elbow.

Kalgrash tripped — but didn't fall. Cords whipped round him.

He was still on his feet, but raveled in seething silver loops. They were all over him.

His armor pinged. Cables were tightening. Plates were weakening.

His helmet wriggled.

They were pulling off his protective shell.

No, worse.

He spluttered — gagged. The tendrils had crawled into the breathing grill. They were prying at his lips.

They were going to slither inside him and pull him apart like thumbs in an orange.

He yanked his arm. He still had his ax, but he couldn't swing it at himself.

The cables jabbed at his eyes.

In another second or two, he'd be blinded. The wire would pierce the soft quick of the eye and start stirring.

And so Kalgrash swung his ax as hard as he could. Not at the cables — he knew he'd never be able to sever so many of them.

But at the ruins of a half-decayed pillar.

His ax hit with a clang.

The pillar collapsed.

And with it, down came a lot of the roof.

TWENTY-SEVEN

A huge pile of broken saint and gargoyle lay on top of Gelt's tendrils. The strands were still looped around the troll, but they were malfunctioning. They were weak and twitching.

"It's like we're holding hands," said Kalgrash, "but this would be a really bad date."

He unwrapped a few cords from around his wrist and threw them to the side. They reared up and then slumped. The weight on them was crushing the life out of them.

"This is the point," said Kalgrash, "where I would excuse myself to go to the bathroom and I would start calling my friends to tell them what a jerk you were."

There was a rattle. As Kalgrash picked off strands, a few plates of his armor had fallen off.

He was not looking good. He was covered in dust, bruised, and, he realized, he was sliced in several places on his arms where the cords had wormed through the mail and started to squeeze.

The troll struggled out of the erratic, flinching loops.

"You think about what you've done, and we'll talk later," he said.

He ran out of the courtyard gate, leaving Gelt trapped and tangled behind him.

Gelt glowered, but could not follow. The monster began rolling the stones off the pile.

Kalgrash worked his way through the house where Brian and he had hidden. "Brian!" he hissed. "Brian! Come here! Come on, if you can crawl! We only have about ten minutes!"

Brian was on his hands and knees, crawling up the stairs.

Kalgrash said, "Did your ancestors go through the whole trouble of natural selection and struggle up out of the muck just so you could crawl again? What are you doing? What would your mother say?"

"I can't see," Brian complained. "I thought it wasn't you."

"Who else would it be? Have you made other plans?"

"You told me to stay put."

"Eh . . . no more staying put. Gelt is boiling mad. He'll be back. We've got to get up to the palace."

He heaved Brian up onto his feet and shuffled the blinded kid through the rooms and into the street.

"Back on the shoulders. Alley-oop."

"Can't I just use the light? Gelt is trapped, you said."

"Temporarily." Kalgrash shrugged. "It's your funeral."

Brian held up the magic lantern and said the Cantrip of Activation.

The street was flooded with light. Grimaces and scowls

191

of stone leaped into relief all around them — furrowed brows and bug eyes and fantastical chins.

The two began running up the hill.

There was no reason to stay out of the avenue now — not with the light on and time ticking while Gelt threw aside the rubble.

The boulevard leading from the cathedral to the quays no longer looked like a dead gala. The rich and intricate facades of the mansions that lined the street could not be seen because of the growths — the gray blobs, propped up with sticks and gutters, that leeched onto the flint and granite.

The growths were all the way up the boulevard — a forest of fungi.

Except, Brian suspected, they weren't fungi at all, but Thusser nests, ready for habitation. These were the luxury units. The cheap suburbs were upstairs, where children hung half devoured by plasterboard walls.

The nests billowed all along the boulevard.

"What are we doing when we get to the palace?" Brian asked. "Do you know where the prison cells are? I don't remember them."

"I know. They're down in the basements."

"They're probably guarded," Brian said. "Maybe by more of those glassy monsters."

"Kreslings. I hate them," Kalgrash said. "They don't kill easy."

They slowed as they approached the belfry of the cathedral and the myriad turrets of the castle. Their breathing came heavily from all the exertion.

Only faintly could the lantern pick out the high towers of the palace, the serpentine pillars and crowded tympanum of the cathedral.

Please may Gregory and Prudence and Snig be in here, Brian thought. *Please may we all get out alive.*

Brian and Kalgrash prepared to cross the drawbridge into the palace.

Then they saw the guards.

The furrowed creatures of smoke and fluid glass stood, waiting, upon the battlements.

With his lantern, Brian made a perfect target. Suddenly, he looked at Kalgrash and saw how well-armored his friend was, and how soft and vulnerable his own human skin was.

I have, he thought in the brief lull before the attack, *so very many inches of face.*

He whispered, "If I don't get through this, you'll free Gregory, right? And try to get those kids out of the walls?"

Kalgrash looked at him, startled.

Perhaps the troll would have answered, had the arrows not started flying.

TWENTY-EIGHT

Four of the kreslings knelt between the crenellations, firing longbows. Several more waited inside the portcullis gate.

Brian threw himself behind the armored troll. He fired his blunderbuss — but missed. The castle's stone teeth fell into the bottomless moat.

"So I stand in front and repel the arrows — and you fire, huh?" Kalgrash asked. "Doesn't that make me, tactically, a wall?"

Brian didn't answer, but crouched behind Kalgrash's knees, speaking the Cantrip of Activation again.

One of the ghastly archers exploded into shards of glass.

Brian trained Old Bess on another. Arrows whistled past his head.

There was a clang from above as one hit the troll's armor. Kalgrash reeled from the strike. Brian ducked and fired again.

Brian had taken out three of the four archers when Kalgrash saw that the drawbridge was going up.

"DRAWBRIDGE!" he yelled. They'd be trapped on the wrong side of the gulf. They'd never be able to get to their friends.

Just visible in the gatehouse, a kresling cranked on a huge lever. Gears turned, pulleys swiveled, and the drawbridge rose.

Kalgrash yelled, *"I SHALL SMITE THEE!"* and hurled himself onto the edge of the drawbridge.

Brian suddenly found himself exposed, with no troll between him and destruction.

The troll landed on his knees and started to slide down the drawbridge, flailing. *"WITH VALOR!"* he added, somewhat after the fact. And then: *"VARLET!"*

Brian darted backward to hide behind a buttress of the cathedral.

The fourth and final archer let fly at Kalgrash as the troll rolled and rattled down the bridge.

From behind the safety of the buttress, Brian aimed carefully at the battlements. He said the Cantrip of Activation.

There was a quick blare of blue fire. No dice. He was too far away to aim accurately. The stone was pocked where the fire had hit it, but no permanent damage had been done.

Kalgrash, meanwhile, faced off with the kresling near the gears. He swung his ax — but the creature thickened when struck. The ax clanged and slid.

The monster snarled and leaped for Kalgrash.

The troll blocked with his ax. The kresling fell.

Kalgrash, smiting left and right, drove the monster back to the edge of the cliff. Below them, the bottomless fissure echoed with their blows.

The claws swiped Kalgrash's arm twice: once, a quick blow to harden the kresling's own hand. By the second strike, the claw was frozen, sharp, and it tore the metal armor to shreds. Kalgrash buckled. His upper arm was deeply gouged. He saw spots. He heard Brian shouting the Cantrip of Activation. Saw blue fire. But Brian could not see him struggle with this monster. The gears were in the way.

The weights had taken over, and the mechanism now labored with no one to crank. Teeth spun and pulleys groaned and the chain flew along in its course.

The monster lunged at Kalgrash again. This time, the kresling's claw knocked Kalgrash to his knees.

The pain from his arm was overwhelming. Through the oozing troll blood, he could see his own gears and rods. He stared stupidly, transfixed.

And then he looked up at his assailant.

And he swung his ax at the monster's knees.

The thing leaped.

But the ax hit the knees.

The knees calcified, freezing the monster in a cheerleader leap.

And the blow, which had struck them clangorously, sent the monster flying backward.

196

The monster couldn't compensate without its legs. It couldn't stop itself from tumbling.

It ricocheted off the edge. It fell into the chasm, smacking the sides.

It shattered as it fell.

Kalgrash stood up. His breathing was labored. He trembled all over. Blood or some hydraulic fluid was swamping his metal sleeve.

He reached up and, exhausted, hauled on the lever to lower the drawbridge.

The gears spun in reverse. The wooden bridge fell.

It was down.

Brian stood at the end of it, the blunderbuss held at the ready, the lantern swaying beneath it. He had destroyed the other creatures of fluid and glass.

Kalgrash, wheezing, gestured. "Come on," he said.

But Brian just stared.

"What?" said Kalgrash.

Brian did not answer, but looked past Kalgrash.

Into the courtyard.

Slowly, Kalgrash turned.

"Hi there, boys," said Milton Deatley. "You both seem real interested in our three-bedroom units. That's great. But I'm afraid they're only for sale to the living. And in a few minutes, I'm afraid that won't be you."

TWENTY-NINE

Brian pointed the blunderbuss at the dead man. He thought of everything that undead Deatley had done: the adults deluded; the children hypnotized; the kids who, terrified, ended up melding into their walls, nothing but fertile ground for the advance of the Thusser Horde. He thought of his friends, stolen from him.

"Take me to them," he said. "Or I'll — I'll destroy you. I'll do it. I'll destroy you."

Milton Deatley smiled and held up his hands. "That's fine. Come with me."

He turned and walked away across the courtyard. Brian walked carefully across the drawbridge. He and Kalgrash followed Deatley into the feasting hall. The light from Brian's lantern dimly gestured at a tapestry on the wall that depicted elfin knights hunting some sniveling, doggish dragon through primeval caverns. Kalgrash groaned with pain. Brian looked at him, alarmed.

Kalgrash explained, "It's an ouchy." He displayed his torn arm. Brian winced in sympathy.

"Come on," said Deatley. The undead developer led them through the kitchens where, centuries before, cooks' boys had hidden nests of fried eels inside whole roast stags, and bakers had painted sweet glaze on confectionary warriors. The spaces were tall, dusty, empty. On the hood of the giant fireplace was carved the Norumbegan coat of arms. Someone more recently had scratched it out.

Kalgrash and Brian went watchfully with their dead host, suspicious of ambush. He led them to the basement stairs.

Deatley asked them, "Did you like the units down on the main boulevard? They're luxury spreads. Really nice. We haven't spared any expense. You and your friends will supply the human element. Rich, rich inner lives we can live off. I think when I arrive here — actually arrive, instead of just driving this corpse around — I'll put a bid on one of the places on the boulevard. It's got all the perks of city living with all the —"

"Be quiet," said Brian. "I'll say the Cantrip of Activation."

"Just thought you'd like to know that you and your friends won't go to waste."

They wound their way down deep beneath the castle. The light from Brian's lantern seemed to huddle in on itself. They walked through vaults where once the collection of imperial wines had been stored, gifts from far-flung duchies, from worlds of fire, from green lands across the sea.

They came, at last, to the dungeons. Bars had been driven into the stone of the pillars and low vaults. A rusty, padlocked door led into the holding cell.

"Your friends," said Milton Deatley, gesturing through the bars. "We're preparing them for colonization. They're particularly fertile ground." He began to undo the heavy locks.

Brian and Kalgrash stared in horror at the three prisoners on the other side. Sniggleping, Prudence, and Gregory were all lying insensate on the stone floor, helmeted, with flashes of light playing across their faces. Of the three, only Prudence still moved. She twitched. Gregory was motionless. His eyes were unblinking.

Brian rushed forward.

Deatley smiled and opened the door for him.

Brian stopped short and gestured with the blunderbuss. "You first," he said.

"Are you sure?" Deatley asked.

Brian's hands shook. The blunderbuss quivered. "Go on," he said.

Deatley said, "I think you want to step in before me."

Brian protested, "Don't — don't try your mind control on me!"

"All right," said Deatley, stepping into the cell. He crossed his arms just inside the door. "But I wasn't trying to use mind control."

"Then it was a stupid suggestion," said Kalgrash. "We weren't born yesterday."

"I just figured that you'd want a little more protection between you and Gelt the Winnower."

At these words, silver cords slapped over Brian's shoulders, wrapped around the blunderbuss, and yanked it from his fingers.

THIRTY

Gelt the Winnower was upon them. He had freed himself and followed them up the hill, into the castle, down to the vaults, and now he hung there, just a few feet behind Kalgrash, surrounded by a halo of darting threads.

The threads came out of his arms, his chest, his legs, and, most disturbingly, his eyes, which were nests of cords. His mouth hung slack, forgotten in the general hunger of his silver feelers.

Against this monstrosity, Brian was unarmed and Kalgrash was one armed. His other, torn severely, drizzled sparks whenever he moved. The battle-ax wobbled in the troll's hands.

It was hopeless. Brian knew that. But this was the only confrontation that could actually slow the Thusser invasion. Deatley and his most dangerous servant had to be defeated. They were the most powerful servitors of the Thusser in the whole alien suburb. If it was hopeless,

Brian figured that he might as well go down with a fight.

And so he lunged past Milton Deatley. He ran to Prudence and began pulling at her camera helmet. The image joggled on its screen. Her mouth opened and closed.

Gelt was gathering his tendrils for a strike against the troll. Kalgrash grunted and raised his ax. Even as he did so, he could feel Milton Deatley's smile behind him.

Gelt's fronds pounced. The troll dodged, skirted around several stout columns.

The Winnower followed, trickling along on loops of wire.

The troll tried his earlier trick — slalom runs through pillars, entanglement. It slowed Gelt, but Gelt was getting wise. The monstrosity set himself down on his own white, ratlike feet, and observed Kalgrash's dodges for a moment, waiting to strike again.

Brian had pulled off Prudence's helmet, but Deatley was at his side, bending down to grab the thing out of his hand.

Brian swung it by its chinstrap. He hit Deatley as hard as he could.

Unfortunately, that was not very hard. Brian was not very strong. Had Deatley been alive, it would barely have bruised him.

Brian swung again, but now Deatley's awful, reconstituted hands were in the way, clutching at him. Prudence didn't stir, but lay by their feet, eyes open, somewhat more at peace.

Deatley seized Brian's shoulders.

Brian panicked and kneed him in the groin.

Evidently, that didn't work anymore. Deatley didn't so much as grunt.

Brian flung the camera (which still shuddered, which still shot out its crazy blasts of color) at the undead man. It struck Deatley softly, forced the corpse back, but didn't do any real damage. Though Deatley did lose his grip on Brian for an instant as he reeled.

Brian staggered toward Gregory.

Gregory's chinstrap was too tight for Brian to pull the helmet off easily. As he struggled, Deatley came in behind him and tried to yank him away from his comatose friend. Brian's fingers slipped on the nylon strap. The old camera whirred and cast brilliant shades across the rough prison walls.

Finally, the strap released. Brian went tumbling backward, taking Deatley with him.

Gregory was free.

But he didn't move at all. The trance was too total.

Brian called their names — "Prudence! Gregory! Prudence, come on!" The two didn't stir.

Milton Deatley stopped wrestling with Brian. He shoved the kid aside and crawled to his feet. He patted at the knees of his suit, wiping off the dust. "You won't wake them up anytime soon," he said. "You have to realize, there is no way you can win. The Thusser Horde is coming. This is to be our age."

"This is our planet," said Brian. "You have no right."

203

"Who's talking about rights? Have you ever seen them exercised? Take the Norumbegans. They claim a right to this castle, this whole kingdom, but they're too weak to even recall their claim. Certainly too weak to stop us from taking what we need." Milton Deatley grabbed Brian's arm and twisted it cruelly. "Only the powerful have rights. The claims of the weak are quickly forgotten."

Brian told himself he would not yelp, though the pain was intense. But Deatley pulled the arm back harder, and Brian couldn't help it.

He screamed in pain and impotent anger. He couldn't stop himself.

He knew, then, the meaning of weakness.

THIRTY-ONE

She saw yellow harvested by workers wearing black sacks, men with rings around their eyes and pointed ears. They watched her so she would not move. She sat in the field of yellow, painted thick as oil pastels, color so rich it crumbled. She waited for them to finish. Purple clouds passed over.

Prudence knew that it wasn't right. It wasn't real.

Everything was darker. She did not like it. She was used to the colors now. Her eyes could not focus. The field was gone. She recalled that it was a dream.

"Prudence! Please! Prudence!"

That was almost certainly her name.

And then she saw feeble light. A lantern or two. Stripes of black.

A stocky boy she knew, standing over her, struggling.

She wondered whether she was supposed to do something now.

Brian saw Prudence blink. Though her face was over-shadowed and hidden partially by her own tangled hair, he saw a look of dawning recognition. He called her name.

"She's waking up," Brian announced to his tormentor. "We're not as easy to confuse as you thought."

"All you're arguing," said Milton Deatley, "is that it's not worth keeping you alive."

He threw the boy down next to the young woman, who coughed and rubbed at her eyes. Brian hit his head badly — saw stars. When he looked up, he could tell the side of his head was bruised and bleeding.

Milton Deatley stood with his back against a pillar. He said, "I'm sorry you're uninterested in becoming a part of the neighborhood. You'd be a particularly fertile resource." He smiled and moved to the cell door. "I'm closing you in now. No one will come back for you. In a few days, you'll be desperate for food and water. Eventu-ally, you'll die of starvation. In a week, the streets in the suburb up above you will be filled with Thusser, newly delivered into this world, strolling about, looking at their fine homes. There is an old Thusser proverb appropriate to this circumstance. It is, unfortunately, too complicated, too nuanced, for you to understand."

And with that, Milton Deatley swung the prison door shut.

The door clanged on Brian's hand. He had made a kind of shambling leap and blocked the bars.

"Give up," said Milton Deatley. "You're not equal to this task."

Kneeling there, with his head throbbing and his hand crunched by a slamming iron grate, Brian did not feel equal to anything. He could hear Kalgrash's yelps as the Winnower snatched at the damaged troll. He looked up at Deatley's raw, mealy face and did not have anything to say.

But a voice, low, gravelly, came from behind him. "No," said the voice, a tortured little scratch of a thing. "No, we're not equal to this. But the Norumbegans are, and I'm putting in a collect call to them right now."

Deatley and Brian looked to the wall, where Prudence was blinking slowly. She held her forehead and muttered.

Deatley scowled, threw the door open, and walked back in. "On what channel?" he demanded. "I'm flooding the channels. Which one? You'll never get through."

Prudence continued to whisper and to tarantula her hand around her head, pressing secret nodes.

"Stop! Stop it!" cried Deatley.

He took a run at her and began to kick her ribs.

At this, Brian, ferocious, heaved himself up and grabbed Deatley. He tangled his arms through the dead man's. The corpse tried to lift him but stumbled. Prudence was still muttering her incantation. Deatley tried to brush Brian off.

And suddenly, Deatley exclaimed, "You're not! You're not calling them! It's a bluff! You don't even know how to call them!"

Prudence smirked. That was a mistake. Deatley growled in irritation and raised his hand to release a burst of magical energy and destroy her utterly.

207

Brian yanked on the developer. The developer's hand was engulfed in fire, ready to fling.

Prudence saw what was coming and screamed.

✳ ✳ ✳

Just outside the cell, Kalgrash was pursued by tendrils. He swiped at them with his ax. He caught a few hard enough to sever them. Most just swayed sideways with his blow.

He could hear Deatley yelling some kind of nonsense, but he couldn't tell what was going on in that corner of the room. He whacked the air with his ax. Nothing seemed to keep the crawling tendrils away.

He ran through a few archways. Gelt was easily able to keep up, shuffling on his dry husks of feet. Gelt grabbed at the troll and seized him.

Kalgrash gasped, wrapped in serpentine coils. He couldn't move. Gelt began to squeeze.

Abruptly, Deatley called, "Gelt! Get rid of this kid! Hold him off for just a second!"

Gelt turned, disengaged several coils from the troll, and shot his tendrils through the bars of the cell. He sought out Brian where he and Deatley fought. Kalgrash helplessly watched the silver cords seek his friend.

Brian felt them brush against him as Gelt felt for who was who. The boy trembled, fighting to keep Deatley from flinging fire at Prudence.

Deatley said three words. Now his whole body glowed. It pulsed with power. He was getting ready to blast them all.

The tendrils poked Brian's face, searched his hair.

Kalgrash ripped his ax backward. It couldn't quite cut the fibers, but it could yank.

Gelt, wrenched, flew toward Kalgrash.

Gelt's jerked tendrils clamped on to Deatley and the pillar, grabbing for an anchor. He couldn't see who he'd trapped.

The troll pulled harder on Gelt, facing away from the battle, like he was dragging a freight train up a hill.

Gelt, helpless, strangled the body of Milton Deatley.

His razor-sharp wires cut the corpse.

Milton Deatley's remains screamed.

Brian pulled away, saw the flickering body rent by metal threads. The blaze of magical energy Deatley had summoned still roamed the man, seething, boiling in the flesh — which bubbled, welts of light popping in the cheeks, the hands, the neck.

Then the Thusser who'd been driving the body abandoned it. Particles spilled around the silver cords — granules of ash and flesh.

The troll yanked again on the Winnower, screaming with the effort.

Blue light now glared through Deatley's sliced limbs, and the eyes, now doubly dead, rolled back. The cords cut deeper, searing with magical discharge. The Winnower mewled, trying to withdraw from the tangle of corpse, clothes, and enchantment. His tentacles stung. He twitched, cutting the dead man deeper —

With a burst, Milton Deatley's body collapsed, released — now sifting like sand — now snapping with energy — now blown across the room — and with a thunderous clap, the man was gone.

Nothing was left of the interdimensional real estate developer but sliced slacks, a jacket, a burned shirt, and year-old dust.

Gelt whined with rage.

Brian, breathing heavily, lacerated by the tentacles that had seized on to him, took stock. He saw his friend the troll being crushed by Gelt. And he saw that Gelt still had the blunderbuss wrapped in a silver wire.

Brian scampered through the door. He flanked Gelt, who was concentrating on Kalgrash. Moving quickly, Brian grabbed the gun. Gelt's silver arm tugged back, but could not change the weapon's direction.

Brian aimed it and spoke the Cantrip of Activation.

There was a blue blast.

The monster, struck, screamed, his silver cords sticking out straight and radiant like a dandelion's needly corona. Brian collected his wits, thought, screamed a word, and fired again.

Gelt the Winnower blew apart. His body collapsed.

His tendrils settled softly to earth like severed webs.

The room, finally, was quiet.

Brian and Kalgrash stared at each other. Both of them were badly damaged. Brian was cut. Kalgrash was slashed. Prudence was wobbling to her feet. Gregory and Snig still lay prone, insensate.

But the fight was over. The Thusser's most powerful servant on Earth was gone.

THIRTY-TWO

In a vaulted cavern beneath a spired palace beneath a towering mountain, a stout boy in glasses leaned over his best friend in the world and slapped him.

Gregory didn't respond. His mouth sagged open slackly. He was breathing, but there was no sign he might wake.

"What do we do?" Brian demanded.

Prudence knelt by his side. "I don't know."

"How's Sniggleping?"

Prudence made a clicking sound with her tongue. "He's a Norumbegan. He'll get over it." She put her hand on Gregory's cheek. "I'm worried Gregory won't. He might be too far in."

Brian, terrified, shook his friend's shoulders. "Gregory!" he yelled. "GREGORY!"

"It's his own fault," said Kalgrash, sitting with his armored knees bunched up by his breastplate. "He wanted to show off his leadership skills. He headed out of the house to save someone who didn't need saving. Sad, sad, sad."

211

Brian frowned. "He was just trying to help."

"He was not trying to help," said Kalgrash, picking at the torn metal of his upper arm. "He's jealous of you. Hey, do you think fiddling with my clockwork will make this wound feel better or worse?"

"Worse," barked Prudence. "Stop it." To Brian, she said, "Slap him again."

"I'll slap him," said Kalgrash.

Brian said, "Kalgrash, don't be so — don't be so mean about him."

"Gimme an egg and I'll give you an omelet. I say turnabout is fair play." Kalgrash folded his arms. "He always wants to be the center of attention. I never liked him. Right from the first time I tried to kill him."

"It was me you swung the ax at."

"Just a little homicide between friends."

Brian was in no mood to smile. Gregory looked pale, maybe even a little blue.

"He's fading," said Prudence. "Gregory!" She leaned into his face. "Gregory, it's your cousin Prudence. We're safe here. There are no Thusser. They're gone. Remember, you're from Brookline, Massachusetts. Your best friend is Brian Thatz." She stroked her cousin's cheek, ran her hand up to his hair, and yanked.

He didn't move.

"You try," said Prudence to Brian.

He said to Gregory, "This is . . . this is your best friend. Brian. We're . . . we've been friends since we were eight. We . . ." His voice caught. He discovered he was almost crying. He looked down at Gregory's pallid, impassive face, nearly the face of a corpse. "We met playing tetherball. You told me to stand near the pole. Then you hit the ball. It took you twenty minutes to untangle me." He said, "Stop thinking about the Thusser. They're not here. Forget about them. They're brainwashing you."

The body was slack. Kalgrash now came forward, concerned, too, and knelt with the others. Brian was glad to see it. Gregory's head lolled.

And suddenly, with the shift of the head, the insensate body began choking.

"Get him up!" Prudence shrieked. "So the spit goes down. . . . Turn his head!"

In his coma, Gregory drowned on his own saliva.

✳ ✳ ✳

He saw that he was clustered about with Thusser. They were everywhere, and had been always. In the streets of cities, on the sidewalks, up staircases three by three. So many of them that he was clamped between their wide shoulders, their dark coats. He couldn't budge. They crushed him. He heard commotion, clamorous as a celebration of the Horde and its power.

Someone was talking about spit.

✳ ✳ ✳

Saliva dripped down Gregory's chin. His eyes stared wide. Involuntarily, his neck bunched and flexed as he

213

choked. "Now lean him forward!" Prudence said. "Drain his mouth!"

* * *

He knew the voices, but did not know whose they were. He could not recall who he was. He felt his breath go out of him.

* * *

"Gregory!" Brian said. He was slapping his friend in the face again. The body was still — no longer choking, but breathing in gasps. "Gregory! It's Brian. You've got to get the Thusser out of your head. Don't think about them!" And suddenly, he remembered Gregory talking about the Cantrip of Activation — saying that if you said not to think about school, the first thing he'd think of was school — and Brian realized he should stop talking about the Thusser entirely. So he began stammering things he knew about his friend: "You . . . you always play jokes on people. You know, with your phone, or stuff taped under someone's seat, or chemicals. People say you're always laughing at something. That's what they say about you. You must . . . must be able to remember.

"You live in a brick house. We used to build stuff in the basement. Robots that didn't work. We wanted to be inventors. You came with my family to Maine. We went fishing. You told me about having a crush on Angelique Maddis. You were . . ."

214

And Gregory's breathing began to quicken, as if he were undertaking some great struggle.

They shook him. They talked to him. They reminded him of excursions to museums, things he'd flung at the television, the pants he wore when he wanted to impress people — "Thanksgiving dinner," said Prudence. "There were only humans there. Only humans. From Connecticut. Remember, Gregory. Our cousin Austin. Our cousin Paul. Actually, he's a pain. Don't remember him. You won't come back."

He started to fade (picturing Thusser carving the turkey, showing their teeth, stripping skin off the bird with their knives).

And then Brian pleaded, "Gregory, come back. We need you." His voice thick, he insisted, "*I* need you, so that we can fight this thing. There are so few of us. Don't leave me here alone. Don't leave me here. I need you to come back."

And at that, Gregory groaned. He struggled with nothing. Kalgrash swiftly moved to make sure the boy's head didn't bruise against the wall. Gregory's legs kicked. He started coughing again.

Brian said, "Please."

And Gregory's eyes focused.

He lifted his head. He looked around.

He was awake.

"Where are they?" he asked.

And Kalgrash said, grimly, "They'll be here soon enough."

THIRTY-THREE

There was a little party in the vault beneath the Palace of Norumbega. There were no hors d'oeuvres, no drinks (except tap water in a Nalgene bottle), no music, no dancing. But that didn't matter. There was more joy in this party than if they'd all been dining at the Ritz. Because, for the moment, they were safe and they were together.

It didn't take much to wake Wee Sniggleping. Prudence just put his head on her knees and said, in a voice cutesy and high, "Oh, isn't he darling! The precious little elfling. Oh, Snig, we'll wake you up like we revived Tinker Bell. Clap, dear children! Clap if you believe in Snig and Tink! Oh, clap, do, little ones, do! Clap for Uncle Snig!" and so on until the old man growled, "Awright, awright, you got me," and opened his surly eyes, pawing at the air in desperation to smother everything adorable. "Terrible to wake from a dream of the Thusser just to discover you're surrounded by mankind." He hawked a loogie on the prison floor. "At least the Thusser have dignity."

216

Gregory, Brian, and Kalgrash told the story of what had happened to them. Prudence gave them big hugs and thanked them for coming to save her.

"You're surprised, aren't you?" said Gregory. "You didn't think we'd make it."

"Oh, I'm surprised, all right," said Prudence.

"See, we're better at this than you thought."

"Yeah, you're amazing," Prudence agreed. "Any time I need someone to sit motionless next to me in a cell for twelve hours, I'll give you a call."

"Hey!" Gregory protested. "That's not fair! I helped Brian with —"

Prudence agreed, "No, you were wonderful. You stare great."

"Where's the thanks?"

"For what? People do more heavy lifting at a teddy bears' picnic."

"Brian," Gregory pleaded, "stand up for me here."

Brian said, "We did it together."

"Isn't he sweet?" Prudence said, ruffling Brian's hair. "Always trying to smooth everything over."

"Would you stop ruffling his hair? What about mine? My hair is totally unruffled!"

Prudence looked at Gregory and coughed. "I'm not sticking my hand in there. Too much product. Your bangs would crackle."

Kalgrash asked, "Does anyone here know how to repair troll arms? I mean, I don't want to interrupt the discussion of gel or anything, but I'm bleeding fake blood all over the real floor."

217

Sniggleping looked at the gash. "I can't repair it," he said. "I'd need a full workshop for that. But I can at least stop the damage from spreading, and — more important — I can turn off the sensation of pain. Nothing easier." He reached into his vest and pulled out a set of little mechanic's tools in felt pockets.

He sat Kalgrash down and got to work.

While Sniggleping labored over the troll's arm, Prudence said, "The Thusser are probably already preparing their next onslaught. We've got to get moving."

"They're completely breaking the Rules," Brian said. "In a few days, they'll start to settle here. We've got to warn the Norumbegans. Like you were pretending to do, Prudence. Honestly, isn't there some kind of a . . . a hotline?"

Prudence shrugged. "I have no idea. I really was bluffing. Snig?"

"Certainly, there was a hotline," said Sniggleping, squinting at a wire he held in his tweezers. "It was in my workshop. But everything there was seized and destroyed. Those are the kind of conditions under which I'm expected to work. So the hotline is gone. Who knows where it's stashed. The only thing left in the area is a sensor. It will send a warning about the arrival of the Thusser, when they come."

"But by then," Brian protested, "it will be too late!"

"Yes. A shame, really," said Sniggleping. "I liked your world. There were several good bits. I particularly liked mist in valleys. Cheese, well aged. Classic-car rallies."

218

Brian insisted, "We've got to convince the Norumbegan Emperor to come enforce the Rules. This place isn't the Thussers'. The mountain is the Norumbegans'. The planet is ours."

Gregory said, "So, yeah, if the big hotline is gone, how are we going to warn the Emperor?"

"The Emperor and all his court are in another world," Sniggleping said. "You'd have to travel there. They all emigrated there when the treaty was struck with the Thusser. If you could find the Emperor's court . . ."

Brian was staring, haunted, into the darkness. He had thought of something. "We can do that," he said. "We can go to their new world."

Gregory asked, "How?"

"Because we found the gate, remember?" Brian said. "It was in the crypt of the cathedral. We couldn't go through at the time. . . ."

"But you could now!" Prudence exclaimed. "I could send you through safely, I bet! Snig? Could we do that?"

Sniggleping nodded and shrugged one shoulder.

"Whoa, wait. Where are we going?" Gregory asked. "We have school on Monday."

"It's probably Monday already," Prudence said. "Or last Monday. Or a month from Monday."

Brian said, "This is more important. If we don't warn the Norumbegans and get them to stop the Thusser, the settlement will start to spread. In a few years, no one will even remember what the world was like without the Thusser."

219

"What do you mean, without them?" Gregory said. "They're all over the place at my house."

Prudence laughed.

Then stopped.

She realized he was serious.

"Come on, they're already in *all* our houses," Gregory said. "You know. Who do you think the guys with the dark rings around their eyes and the pointy ears are? In the mini-mart, Brian, you know. They stand by the Little Debbie products. Two of them. Or at the fire station. They're always standing on either side of the garage doors. You know what I'm talking about. Don't look at me like that! They walk down Beacon Street in a formation all the time."

"No," said Brian, softly. "No, Gregory, they don't. Not yet."

"Unless," Prudence said, "he's seeing something that's happened since you came here. If time is different."

Brian realized she could be right. "They can't be," he said. "They . . ." He didn't finish the thought.

"We've got to go," said Kalgrash. "Quickly. Where's this portal?"

"In the crypt of St. Diancecht's Cathedral," Brian answered quietly.

And so they walked up through the castle and to the cathedral. This time, there were no monstrous humanoids to menace them. The kitchens were silent. The feasting hall was empty, except for the pageantry of the hunt upon the wall. If there were any more kreslings, they had evidently abandoned the courtyard and the battlements.

Brian crossed the drawbridge with his blunderbuss at the ready, and no one threatened them.

In the crypt of the cathedral they passed down the line of Emperors, from the first kings who arrived from a realm across the sea in a flying coracle to those who'd built the towers and deeps of the subterranean kingdom to the final, dissipated monarchs, who had collected wines and played tennis while the Thusser had gained in power. Each Emperor lay upon his bier, carved in stone, until the last. That final one sat up upon his sarcophagus, his gown falling off his shoulder, staring into the darkness as if awakened from a nightmare. Or into one.

The last Emperor gazed through an arch, over which was carved in crude letters the English words *Stay Out*.

"Last time," said Brian, "monsters attacked us when we tried to go through there."

Sniggleping nodded sourly. "Guardians of the Gate. You and Jack Stimple destroyed them. There was a fire."

The five of them walked through the arch. There was an awful stench of decay in the room. Moldering, brittle black rags covered the floor — the remains of creatures that once protected the gate through which the Norumbegans had fled, centuries before.

The gate itself was a panel of darkness. The eye could not determine whether it was flat or an absence. It was simply black.

"I'll stabilize the gate for you," said Prudence.

Brian asked, "You can't come through with us?"

"No," said Prudence. "You need us here to hold the gate open." She smiled. "Hurry back," she said. "I'm really hungry. I could really do with a vegetable curry right about now."

"What use is sorcery," said Gregory, "if you can't magic up a vegetable curry?"

Prudence walked to the wall of darkness. "Snig?" she said. "I don't know exactly how to work the portal. The only ones I've used were local. I've never seen one this complicated before." There were little symbols and cranks around the gate. Sniggleping walked forward and explained the workings of the thing to Prudence. Together, they reached up to each rune, each crank, and they twisted the levers and touched the runes and adjusted dials. Sniggleping whispered words to himself.

The quality of absolute darkness subtly changed.

Sniggleping nodded.

"Ready?" said Prudence.

"It is. But I don't know if they are," said Sniggleping, gesturing at the boys. He stepped back. "The gate is open and should lead directly to the Norumbegans' new world."

"All right," said Prudence to the boys and their troll. "We'll guard the pass. You go through. Find the Emperor and warn him that it's now or never. The Norumbegans have to come back now."

Brian, Gregory, and Kalgrash hesitated. They stood before the curious darkness.

"Trying to go through that gate . . ." Kalgrash said. "It's kind of like making up your mind to swim in the river in the midwinter. You know, I never can decide whether to wade in or cannonball."

222

Gregory said, "I usually go in backward. I don't know why that helps, but it does."

"You've done a great job so far," said Prudence. "I believe we can all do this. We've just got to keep working together."

Brian said, "What else are we going to do?"

Kalgrash swept his hands forward. He said, "Alley-oop."

With that, they walked forward. Brian turned and waved. Prudence waved back at him. He stepped forward and was engulfed. His friends were already gone. They passed through the wall into another world.

Prudence and Sniggleping watched them go. They stood amidst the clutter of charred monster, arms crossed.

"Good luck to them," said Sniggleping. "Good luck, I say." He reached into his vest pocket again and drew out some playing cards.

For some hours, Prudence and he played piquet. There, in that crypt, beneath that lost cathedral, in that abandoned city, under that eldritch mountain, ringed by networks of streets and culs-de-sac and faux lanterns and lawns, the two sat through the hours.

They flipped discards and awaited the return of ancient kings.

ABOUT THE AUTHOR

M. T. Anderson is the author of *The Game of Sunken Places*, the National Book Award–winning Printz Honor book *The Astonishing Life of Octavian Nothing, Traitor to the Nation, Volume I: The Pox Party*, the Printz Honor book *The Astonishing Life of Octavian Nothing, Traitor to the Nation, Volume II: The Kingdom on the Waves, Feed, and Thirsty.* He lives in Cambridge, Massachusetts, when not trolling the forests of Vermont for inspiration.

A special sneak preview of M. T. Anderson's

Coming soon!

A ceremonial staircase led to nowhere. It stood in the middle of a rough, broken plain. A stocky boy sat on the stairs, sagging low, his elbows on his knees. A dim blue light shone from jagged cracks in the black sky. It faintly lit a cluster of ruins.

Brian Thatz raised his head to look out across the murky horizon. Arches below him supported nothing. Columns stood with no roof. Cellars sat naked to the elements. And beyond all this, there was only the slime.

Brian uncurled, reached out to lift the singed leg of a broken chair, and stirred the ashes of his fire. The ashes glowed faintly. He slid across the step he sat on to get closer to the warmth.

At the top of the staircase lay a black slab, a gateway to another world.

Brian was cold — chilled to the bone — and tired. He had not eaten for a day. At least he thought it was a day. Time was difficult, for there was no sun, no night, no day — just cracks in the sky and the glimmer of far marshes of stew.

The ruins covered a square mile or so. They were all built of rough-hewn brown stone. Hardly anything stood. Foundations. A few walls. The staircase was the tallest thing in the city. It was a broad staircase, and had a twist to it. In an earlier age, all the refugees of lost Norumbega had fled down these wide steps, coming to this world to make a new home.

Now a dull silence lay over the fallen metropolis. Occasionally, the wind stirred, shuffling over the desolate marshes.

Brian could hear the bickering of his friends as they returned to the camp.

"This is dumb."

"*You're* dumb."

"I am not dumb."

"I didn't mean you were actually dumb. I just mean it's dumb to say that things are dumb."

"You're not even — don't even argue with me! You're not even real!"

"So I'm fake, and you're dumb. We're even."

"You're dumb *and* fake. You're programmed to be dumb."

Brian was exhausted and wished they'd stop fighting. They had all spent the last twelve hours or so searching the ruins for life or clues. Before that, they'd spent an awful day crawling around under a mountain, dodging silver tentacles, defending a kitchen against alien invasion, and vanquishing an undead real estate developer.

Brian's friends came trudging up the steps to nowhere. One was a blond boy with a burned hand wrapped in a piece of cloth. The other was a troll in Renaissance armor.

"We didn't find anything," said Kalgrash, the troll.

"We found *something*," said Gregory, the boy. "A bureau. We found a smashed-up bureau."

Kalgrash held out a wooden drawer. "For firewood." He tossed it down on the step. It cracked and slid down a few stairs.

Brian stood up and looked out over the sinkholes and slime. "What are we going to do? Where have they all gone?"

The three had risked everything to come in search of the Norumbegans, the elfin race that had raised this city in this weird plain. Back in the pleasant valleys of Vermont, the tricky, wicked Thusser had been arranging an alien settlement, stealing into dreams, and corrupting time. The Thusser's invasion had been slowed, Brian hoped, by the destruction of their agent on Earth — but it had not been stopped. Even as Brian stood helplessly on this staircase to nowhere, the Thusser might be marching through a gateway onto the green lawns of Brian and Gregory's world.

"No bodies," said Kalgrash, squinting. He clanked over to the side of the staircase and looked down at the cellars. "No sign of a battle or fire."

"The bureau was almost okay," said Gregory. "Just missing one leg. It was, you know, the kind of bureau that has legs."

"Maybe," said Kalgrash softly, "maybe the city was never destroyed."

"What do you mean?" Brian asked.

"I don't think the city was ever finished in the first place."

Brian and Gregory thought about this. The wind picked up. It blew Brian's black hair into his eyes, and he raised his hand to push the mess of it back.

Kalgrash said, "Maybe it's not ruined. Maybe it's unbuilt. Like the Norumbegans abandoned it. They got here, started to build — *tinka-tonka, tinka-tonka, tinka-tonka* — and then they moved on. Nothing looks like it was ever finished. I mean, the stonework. In the City of Gargoyles, they did all this fancy carving. Here, nothing's carved. It's like they were just starting. And I think some of these aren't even cellars — they're quarries. Where they were cutting out the rock. Yup." He nodded and looked around at the pits and columns. "Yup, yup, yup. That's what I think."

Gregory sat down wearily by the fire. He rubbed his roughly bandaged hand.

"I think you're right," said Brian. "Yeah."

Kalgrash mused anxiously, "I wonder what made them keep going . . . or . . . you know . . . wiped them out."

"It doesn't matter," said Gregory. "The thing is, we're trapped, right?"

"Yeah," said Brian. "Prudence and Snig can get us through the portal on their side, but we need someone to open it from this end, too. I don't know how."

"Right. Bingo," said Gregory. "So it doesn't really matter whether the Norumbegans were wiped out or they left. Because either way, we're stuck here in the middle of nowhere with nothing to eat and nothing in any direction except an ocean of goo." He flapped his hand at the glistening swamp.

"Better goo than gunk," said Kalgrash.

"What?" Gregory said, exasperated.

"Gunk's grimier than goo. Goo's . . . gookier, but not grimy." Kalgrash looked to Brian for support. "Am I wrong?"

Brian didn't answer. He was looking up at the obsidian portal, which just twelve hours before they had walked through like it was a pool, but which now, if they tried to pass back through, would be hard as marble.

Gregory glared at them both. He picked up the broken drawer and snapped it across his knee. He fed the pieces into the failing fire.

The black smoke went up, curled like the staircase, rising high above the shattered landscape and disappearing into the gloom.